THE LAIRD'S KISS
HIGHLAND LAIRDS

ELIZA KNIGHT

ABOUT THE BOOK

Highland warrior Laird Ian Sinclair longs for adventure. After a lengthy time north in the Orkney Isles, he agrees to undertake a rescue mission at his brother's behest. Crossing the English border to retrieve Lady Rhiannon is not going to be easy and could prove deadly. Eager for the daring challenge, Ian dodges the enemy's sword to see his task through. What he doesn't expect is the lady he's charged with protecting is feisty and beautiful—and he has a sudden strong desire to claim her.

Desperate to escape the oppressive rule and depressing future she faces at the hands of her estranged brother, Rhiannon had written her cousin in Scotland, begging for help. When aid arrives, Rhiannon is surprised to find her rescuer is no more than a rogue with a terrible plan. But what choice does she have? She must trust her cousin—and the wild, handsome Scot who promises her safety.

As they race across the border, thwarting her brother's men, Ian must resist the urge to wrap the lady in his arms.

Rhiannon finds herself falling hard for the laird, who is willing to risk everything to keep her safe. The pull between them intensifies, and denying their desire gets harder. Surrendering to passion will leave them vulnerable to the enemy. Are they willing to risk death for love's sweet embrace?

JANUARY 2024

Cover Design by Dar Albert

Edited by Erica Monroe

MORE BOOKS BY ELIZA KNIGHT

Highland Lairds

The Laird's Prize
The Laird's Kiss - pre-order!
The Laird's Guardian Angel - coming soon

Distinguished Scots

A Scot's Pride
A Dash of Scot - pre-order!
A Scot's Perfect Match - coming soon

Scots of Honor

Return of the Scot
The Scot is Hers
Taming the Scot

Prince Charlie's Rebels

The Highlander Who Stole Christmas
Pretty in Plaid

Prince Charlie's Angels

The Rebel Wears Plaid
Truly Madly Plaid
You've Got Plaid

The Sutherland Legacy

The Highlander's Gift
The Highlander's Quest
The Highlander's Stolen Bride
The Highlander's Hellion
The Highlander's Secret Vow
The Highlander's Enchantment

The Stolen Bride Series

The Highlander's Temptation
The Highlander's Reward
The Highlander's Conquest
The Highlander's Lady
The Highlander's Warrior Bride
The Highlander's Triumph
The Highlander's Sin
Wild Highland Mistletoe (a Stolen Bride winter novella)
The Highlander's Charm (a Stolen Bride novella)
A Kilted Christmas Wish – a contemporary Holiday spin-off
The Highlander's Surrender
The Highlander's Dare

The Conquered Bride Series

Conquered by the Highlander
Seduced by the Laird
Taken by the Highlander (a Conquered bride novella)
Claimed by the Warrior
Stolen by the Laird
Protected by the Laird (a Conquered bride novella)
Guarded by the Warrior

The MacDougall Legacy Series

Laird of Shadows
Laird of Twilight
Laird of Darkness

Pirates of Britannia: Devils of the Deep

Savage of the Sea
The Sea Devil
A Pirate's Bounty

THE THISTLES AND ROSES SERIES

Promise of a Knight
Eternally Bound
Breath from the Sea

The Highland Bound Series (Erotic time-travel)

Behind the Plaid
Bared to the Laird

Ancient Historical Fiction

A Day of Fire: a novel of Pompeii
A Year of Ravens: a novel of Boudica's Rebellion

French Revolution

Ribbons of Scarlet: a novel of the French Revolution

L ady Rhiannon Dacre jiggled the cold iron handle of her bedchamber for what had to have been the one-hundredth time, with the same result as the previous tries. The door was locked.

"This is ridiculous," she growled at the unbudging door, giving it a mighty slap that reverberated through her arm and tingled uncomfortably in her elbow.

Locked away, a prisoner in her own home. This was her brother Adam's doing, a new tactic to show his control over her. The idiot could exert as much power as he wanted, but he'd never see her cower. And he'd also never see her relent to his demands, especially when she barely knew him. The idea that he believed he could march into her life and decide her fate was ludicrous.

Besides, she'd now been able to sneak a third letter out of the castle via the servants who were sympathetic to her plight. She was certain at least one of them would reach her cousin, Douglass Sinclair, Lady Caithness, in the Highlands of Scotland, where she lived with her husband, the Earl of Caithness. If her brother wasn't going to let her out until she agreed to do his bidding, then she needed to escape on her own.

All three letters had been approximately the same:

Dearest Cousin,

I hope this message finds you well. And I wish it were with good tidings that I sent it. But alas, I must implore you for help. While you were away, my brother retrieved me from Appleby and locked me away in his dank, depressing castle. How I long for your company. I know you must be very busy with your new life and your husband, but I do not know who else to turn to. My brother plans to marry me off come spring to one of his vile comrades who has been traveling abroad and will return then. It is not a marriage befitting of my station, which wouldn't bother me if it were for love, but instead, it is to repay a debt he owes this man. I pray this missive reaches you before my fate is sealed. And I pray that there is some way you may be able to help me.

I wrote to your father, but his message was returned as he is on campaign for the king and was unable to receive it.

I do not know how you could help me, but even a letter back would brighten my day.

Your loving cousin,

Rhiannon

Perhaps if she'd grown up under lock and key or even in the same household as her brother, she might have been more afraid of what he was capable of. But she'd been lucky to grow up with Douglass in her uncle's household at Appleby Castle, not too far from where she was now at Dacre Castle. It had almost been as if she had a real family she could count on, not this insanity her brother was subjecting her to.

After all, since when did brothers lock their sisters in their rooms? Well, perhaps that was a silly question as she was certain not to be the first. All the same, Adam was locking the wrong door, and she would make him pay for it.

After she escaped.

Rhiannon grabbed the handle of the door and jiggled it violently, groaning in frustration when it still refused to budge. "You cannot keep me locked in here," she shouted with a voice that was growing weaker and a throat sorer than it had been the day before.

Their parents, God rest their souls, had died when she was a little girl. At the time of their passing, she'd been too young to be of interest to her brother for anything; he'd found her a nuisance, which was why she'd been sent to Appleby in the first place. He'd taken over Dacre, and she'd thought he had been happy to do so. But as soon as Douglass had been whisked off to Scotland to be married, Rhiannon had found herself alone, and her brother had come pounding at the Appleby Castle door late one night.

Goosie, her cat, had leapt up from where she'd been asleep in the crook of Rhiannon's bent knees as the entire castle had reverberated from the sound. The guards at the gate had apparently let her brother in, but no one had been awake to unbar Appleby's doors. She rather liked that he'd had to wait, even if it only made matters worse when she finally saw him.

She'd been so groggy when the servants had alerted her to a visitor that it had been hard to figure out exactly what was happening, and she supposed that was what Adam had wanted. To create confusion and chaos by showing up in the dead of night.

He'd swept into the castle and demanded she return with him. The servants and guards of Appleby had no chance of helping her as her brother was theoretically her guardian, though he'd shirked his duties long enough she had thought there was some loophole that would nullify his orders concerning her.

The problem was that she only had a few guards, and her brother had arrived with an army.

All the seneschal could say to her was that when her uncle returned, he would be sure to fetch her. The seneschal would relay her messages, and she would be back with her uncle before any time had passed. Not exactly the most comforting statement, but the only thing she could rely on. There was no other choice.

But that had been months ago. Months of being held inside this castle. And now, because she'd threatened to run, she'd been locked inside this chamber, only allowed to walk about outside under guard—and only if her brother deemed it worthy enough to remember her existence.

Which, sadly, he seemed to feel her existence most of the time was optional.

And how she wished she had Goosie with her now. Poor cat, alone somewhere in the castle or even locked outside. With another frustrated growl, she grabbed the small dagger she kept on the table at her bedside—something her uncle had encouraged her and her cousin to do, the last line of defense should their walls be breached—and whirled around to face the door that kept her from escaping. She hurled the dagger toward the planks with a mighty heave, retrieved it, and threw it again. And again. And again.

With every inch, the dagger drew closer to the mark she'd made in her mind—the precise location of her brother's head should he finally deign to open the door. She willed the door to open before the blade struck, her brother on the other side where it lodged instead.

But the door didn't open, and the blade stuck in the center of the door with a loud *thunk*, mocking her desire for revenge and a good escape.

Rhiannon prided herself on being skilled with daggers. Her uncle had seen to it that she and her cousin Douglass were well trained in self-defense, especially with a dagger, which he seemed to think would surprise any wolves in sheep's clothing who dared attack them. Savage beasties, he'd called them when she and Douglass really got going, looking at them with pride in his eyes.

Of course, if she wasn't afraid of being hanged, burned, or beheaded, she might murder the man who dared call himself her brother. Adam was a fool and a stranger to her. Yet as much as she dreamed of her dagger making its mark, the truth was she wasn't a murderer, and these thoughts of bloodshed were relatively new in her life.

But who could blame her? Being kept a prisoner would make anyone want to do away with their jailer. Estranged brother or not.

Still, out of respect for her parents, whom she'd loved, some small part of her felt obligated to Adam. By blood or by an unforeseen connection. Maybe it was because she knew they shared parents—a mother and father whose memories felt as if they were fading away faster than a short gust of wind—that she wanted to know her brother. To like him. To get along. He was the only connection she had to the parents she'd lost. Perhaps he would be able to share with her memories of his own about their parents so she might get to know them better through his eyes.

"Adam!" she shouted through the door, slamming her hands against it, wincing at the pain of having rubbed the skin raw with her pounding. "Let me out!"

Her pleas for release were a daily mantra since he'd started locking her in here and one that was slowly making her go mad—in addition to her voice now being all crackly.

Footsteps sounded outside the door, and she backed up several paces, watching the handle to see if it would shift downward. Praying that it would move. Willing whoever was on the other side to let her out, let her out, *let her out*!

There was a slight jingle, the sound of keys, and then the very distinct sounds of the door being unlocked. The click and grind echoed in the silent chamber.

Seconds later, Adam was staring right at her, the hard angles of his face—so unfairly like their father's—rigid, not a loving bone in his body, nor a care when he stared right at her. While she kept in the back of her mind that he was her blood relative, her brother, it did not appear that Adam harbored the same familial emotions.

"You're acting like a madwoman." His voice was harsh, and his lips curled with disgust.

"You locked me in here like a madman," she retorted.

"Because you've threatened to run away." He said it as if he were explaining to a toddler how the world works.

Rhiannon gritted her teeth. "Because you're trying to marry me off to that blackguard."

Adam gritted his teeth right back. "That blackguard is *my friend*."

Rhiannon cocked her head to the side, pursing her lips and giving her brother a look that said she didn't believe a word he said. "Is he, though?"

The muscle in the side of Adam's jaw flexed, and when he next spoke, his voice was harder than before. "He is, and you'll respect my decision and the union."

Rhiannon held back a grimace. "You make it hard to respect you. I barely know you, and the minute you reappeared back into my life, it was with harsh words and cruelty."

Adam laughed, the sound grating. What she wouldn't give to return to her uncle's castle and never set her eyes on her brother again.

"Cruelty?" he said. "You don't know the half of it. You grew up spoiled with Uncle, and now you think the world owes you something. 'Tis about high time you learned the place of women in society. You are chattel. Nothing more than a vessel to carry the heirs of the man you wed."

If he'd slapped her, she might have been less shocked. "I pity the woman who is forced to marry you."

Rhiannon held her brother's gaze, her head high, waiting for Adam to retaliate.

"You will behave," was all he said, and she supposed she should be grateful that he hadn't laid hands on her. Not now, and not ever. His cruelty was different. His cruelty meant he took her freedom and forced her to wed a man demanding payment for gambling debts—she was little more than chattel. A payment for her brother's disastrous habit.

The man Adam had demanded she marry was not one her parents or her uncle would have chosen for her. Born into nobility, she'd been groomed her whole life to take up a position as mistress to some grand castle or house. Now, she'd be relegated to wife of a gambler, a man who claimed to be a merchant but whose true income lay in lending money to men who had no hopes of winning, and then charging interest. Scrubbing the floors and cooking meals while birthing babies from a man she didn't love and who, in turn, didn't love her was not a life she wanted to be consigned to. And that was the exact impression her brother had given her of her new future. All to pay his balance. She didn't even know what kind of "merchant" her future husband was.

The only information Adam had felt necessary to share was that she was the payment for a sizable debt her brother owed. Oh, how far they'd fallen. If her parents knew what was happening, they'd roll in their graves, and she wouldn't blame them. Uncle, if he were here, would have laughed in Adam's face.

She was rolling on the inside, her stomach twisting into a thousand knots, and trying not to vomit.

"I hate you," she said, all the venom she felt pushing out of her in a breath.

Adam laughed and rolled his eyes. "You're a petulant child. Your husband will teach you your place, and then maybe you'll learn to have respect and show it when it's due."

Rhiannon bit her tongue when she wanted to start screaming at him. To rush him and shove him and force her way out the door, but she knew doing that wouldn't help her situation in the least. Her brother was easily six inches taller and several stone heavier. She might have the element of surprise, but he would quickly be able to overpower her, and then where would she be?

Locked in the room again.

So, instead, Rhiannon changed tactics. It appeared Adam did not react well to anger. Perhaps softness was what he needed to be swayed. She ducked her chin and said, "Fine. I will learn respect. I'm sorry for being so...obstinate. In a show of mercy, will you please let me outside for just a short walk? At least to get Goosie. She must be beside herself without me. Have your strongest and fastest guards follow me if you don't trust me, but I need air. If I wither away in this chamber, I will be worth nothing to you or the man you've promised me to."

She kept her face as meek looking as she possibly could, an expression that was unnatural for her. But Adam, who knew his horse better than he knew her, didn't pick up on her pretenses. Perhaps he thought so highly of himself that his will alone would have subdued her in such a quick fashion. My God, his idiocy knew no bounds.

Adam let out a massive sigh and stared at her as if she were a lost child in need of a home—which she kind of was at the moment, hoping Douglass would come through for her.

"You poor thing," he said. "And that stupid pet of yours. The manners they taught you at Appleby are atrocious. But I suppose that should be expected. Uncle was always weak, and Douglass was always a spoiled brat."

Rhiannon nodded, folding her hands demurely in front of her because she wasn't giving up on her ploy to get outside, even if it meant selling her soul to the devil in front of her. She didn't believe a word he said. And he could try to spin it a million different ways, and she never would believe him or the words coming from his mouth. Besides, her poor pet, however ridiculous her brother thought Goosie to be, could be lost and scared or hurt. And if Rhiannon needed to pose a few minutes longer as a demure lady, that was all right as long as it got her what she wanted.

She waited, counting down the seconds in her mind as her brother took an interminably long time to deliberate his options.

"Very well, I suppose. Come along then."

Rhiannon quickly ducked her head to keep from showing shock at his easy acceptance of her acting. This was too easy. There had to be some trick going on. But when she chanced a glance in his direction, he turned his back on her and beckoned her to follow him out of the chamber.

She kept her hands folded in front of her, her head down as they passed through the corridor and descended the thin winding stairs to the great hall where servants set out the morning meal, which she'd not been invited to. An hour or so ago—hard to tell because she had no way of keeping time—someone had brought her bowl of lukewarm porridge and a cup of milk that tasted a day away from going sour. Like a true prisoner. What had her brother instructed these people about her? That she was to be treated like rubbish? Not all of the servants were loyal to her, and she couldn't blame them. Adam's punishments were harsh.

"Go on, outside with you." He waved her toward the door, then flicked his fingers in the direction of one of his guards to follow. The guard rolled his eyes, obviously irritated that he'd been put on watch.

As she passed through the door, one of the maids, an older woman she recognized from her childhood, smiled at her cautiously and offered a subtle wink. She'd been the one Rhiannon had asked to send out her last letter a few weeks ago, and she hadn't seen the maid since. That was the sign she was looking for that it had been done.

Rhiannon was tremendously grateful the woman hadn't been caught and punished as she had feared. Relief washed over her, and a sudden weight lifted from her chest. The servant was safe, her message was on its way and would soon be in Douglass's hands. Now, all she had to do was pray that the letter arrived to her cousin in time—because if rescue didn't arrive until after she'd been forced to say her vows, then there was no help for her.

Outside, the sun felt foreign. Rhiannon paused a moment, closing her eyes and tilting her face toward the sky to feel that soft warmth of the air on her skin. How long had it been since her brother had last allowed her out of the castle? At least a fortnight, if not longer. With her senses keen for the jingle of a bell around Goosie's neck, she listened. Over two weeks without her meant so many predators could have gotten to her sweet pet.

She walked toward the gate, snapping her fingers and making the subtle call with the click of her tongue that usually had Goosie running. The guard didn't say a word, not even as she passed under the gate and out into the fields dotted with flowers. Goosie often hunted in the fields, looking for a mouse or other tiny rodent to devour. A glance back saw that the guard wasn't paying attention to her, his gaze on the women washing by the distant burn. He had no doubts that she would stay here and he wouldn't have to chase her. Incredibly arrogant of him.

But he wasn't wrong. She had no supplies, and her knife was still sticking out of the back of her bedroom door. Rhiannon wanted to run, but doing so without a weapon and without at least a day or two of food—let alone without her cloak for sleeping in the chill of the night out of doors—was setting herself up for disaster.

But she could pretend. Daydreams flashed in her mind's eye and made her smile a little at the thoughts.

Another cluck of her tongue, and she could have sworn she heard the tinkling of a bell. She paused, slightly tilting her head to listen. Then she moved toward the sound. She hoped it wasn't phantom bells ringing.

The closer they drew to the forest that dotted the left side of the castle, the closer her guard stepped to her, now suddenly a little more alert. She didn't usually wander this far, and doing so must be prickling his senses.

To be fair, Rhiannon was teasing him to a point to see how far she could go in the forest and get away with it, and the guard was too stubborn and arrogant to warn her to come back. But also, she thought she heard the distant meow of

Goosie, and she wasn't going to give up the search for her beloved cat.

The jingling grew closer, and the guard said, "Halt, lady."

She ignored him with a glance, and when he touched his hand to the hilt of his sword, she lifted her brow at him and stopped.

"Are you planning to do something with that weapon, sir? Or are you afraid of a wee feline?"

"What?" he sputtered. "No."

"Then get your hand off your sword."

He frowned but did as she said.

"If that is my cat, Goosie is harmless. And if you think I'm running away, you must know that I'm not. Besides looking for my cat, I'm searching for a few wild onions or mushrooms or the like. They will add flavor to Cook's meals that I'm sure everyone would enjoy. So don't think I'm running away. I can assure you that was merely me sputtering in a fit of female weakness. I know my place."

Despite her lying through her teeth and the hint of derision in her voice, the guard smiled and nodded, appeased. Goosie had yet to appear, but Rhiannon felt eyes watching her. Likely, as soon as she knelt to start picking the mushrooms, her cat would pounce in a game they often played.

Rhiannon had to turn away from her guard, so he didn't see her roll her eyes as she marched into the forest on the pretense of finding some wild vegetables. Of course, she'd never found any before because she had no idea what they looked like, and she was more likely to poison someone with her finds than to offer them any culinary inspiration.

But what the guard didn't know wouldn't hurt him. The real reason she'd wanted to come into the forest today was to plan her escape—she needed to memorize the various hiding places and escape routes.

She'd noticed her brother didn't have a regular guard

stationed on this part of the woods, though they did usually circle around her for their morning and evening rounds. But on the right side, where the road led toward the village, they always had two guards on duty in case someone came toward the castle.

She suspected it was because her brother feared the men that he was indebted to more than he feared a siege from a neighboring army.

They'd made it no more than a couple dozen paces into the woods when a giant of a man stepped out from behind a massive tree so huge it could have easily fit ten of her inside its trunk. No wonder he'd been able to hide so easily. Rhiannon halted so fast that she nearly fell backward.

The man watched her steadily, his eyes the color of a blue sea in a storm. Dark hair framed his face. He looked just as casual as if they'd happened upon him taking a stroll. But no one simply took a stroll in the woods, especially not on another man's land.

There was an air of danger that surrounded him. The sheer size of him was enough to make her gape. And beneath his simple clothes, muscles bulged, exuding a power that proclaimed he could break her in half if he wanted.

He kept one of his hands behind his back, concealing something. A giant sword? An axe?

She waited for more men to slip out from the hiding place, but he appeared to be alone, though she didn't trust that.

"You're on Dacre lands," her guard said, hand on the hilt of his sword again.

Oddly, Rhiannon didn't feel as afraid as she thought she should feel at the sight of the warrior. More like mildly annoyed. Though it should have been terrifying to find him here in the woods, there was something calming about the lines of his face.

But his presence did put a damper on her plans. She wasn't going to be allowed out for any more walks after this. Her brother would forbid it. And this stranger had likely scared Goosie away. Now, she'd probably not see her poor cat for another fortnight unless her brother showed her mercy.

She frowned at the intruder.

"I know where I am," he said with a Scottish burr that surprised her given his rather English attire of plain breeches and a shirt—both of which she tried to ignore hid his bulging muscles. "I came on purpose."

A Scot? And he'd come here on purpose? How fascinating.

"Then you'd best be on your way," the guard said. "We're not expecting anyone today. And especially not any savages."

But the Scotsman only grinned, and then his eyes found hers. "'Tis my lucky day." He pulled his arm from behind his back to show a black cat with a red ribbon and a bell around her neck.

Goosie.

2

There might have been a small part of Ian Sinclair that was a glutton for punishment or maybe completely mad, for he lived for moments like this. When danger pressed in all around, the thrill of a fight on the cusp of the next breath. The physical exertion and the peril made him smile.

And though he was certain he could beat the English guard standing in front of him—who was trying to look as if he wasn't about to piss himself in the name of protecting a woman that he obviously didn't respect—if it came down to it, there was always the chance that Ian wouldn't harm a hair on the dolt's head. Because he held all the power of knowing his purpose, and he'd surprised them with his appearance.

Of course, there was always the chance he was wrong in making the assumption. That the guard would get the jump on him or that the lass would somehow surprise him by pulling out a dagger and slipping it between his ribs without his notice.

But it was not knowing what was going to happen that

thrilled him. That spark of danger that could blaze into an inferno. Ian lived for a good adventure.

It was one of the reasons why he'd decided to help his brother in fetching this lass. And he was fairly certain it was her. Ian's sister-by-marriage, Douglass, had distinctly described Lady Rhiannon, and the woman standing before him fit perfectly. Down to the look of defiance in her blue eyes that dared him to do anything. Red-gold hair, tall, lithe— though Douglass hadn't mentioned the curves that drew Ian's eyes.

What made him smile was that he had made a wild guess about the cat, and the look in Rhiannon's eyes said as much— the feline belonged to her. She'd been making some clicking sounds with her tongue, and who made sounds like that unless they were looking for a pet?

"Your lucky day?" she asked him, a delicate hand reaching for the feline who seemed content to stay in his arms. "I say it's mine, as it seems you found Goosie. Give her here."

Bossy. Ian was certain the look she passed him was meant to be haughty, and if he were any other man, he might have taken it that way. But he wasn't any other man. And he had two haughty sisters at home who had shown plenty of bravado, including sweet Iliana, who'd no sooner bake a cake than gut a man.

"To have come across the two of ye," Ian said, adding a wink to throw them off, "is luck. And more so to have located what ye seem to have lost."

As a show of good faith, Ian did let the cat down. Goosie, as the lass had called her, gave his leg a little stroke with her tail before trotting over to the lass, bell jangling. The cat wove around Rhiannon's skirted legs with a purr, looking at him with what he assumed might be feline gratitude. Hard to say; it was a cat, after all.

"Have you lost your way?" the lass asked, and Ian couldn't be sure if she were talking to him or Goosie.

Before she could bend down to lift the black ball of jingling fur, her guard grasped her arm and shoved her behind him. Poor lad. The cat gave an irritated hiss and swiped at the guard's boots, leaving little scratch marks on the leather.

"Don't speak to this barbarian," the guard said. "He's clearly lost his way by several hundred miles. I suggest you turn around now, heathen, and head back the way you came."

"Good idea," Ian said, grinning mischievously.

The guard was playing right into his hands. The poor welp had droplets of sweat forming on his brow, a sure sign of his nerves. His voice pitch had risen a notch as well. Truly, it wouldn't be fair for him to take the lad on in a fight. Like a lion swiping at a cub.

"Though, if I didna return with the package I seek, I'll be asking for trouble."

"Package?" the guard asked cautiously, while the lass who had moved to stand beside her guard rather than behind eyed him intelligently.

"Aye." Ian loved a good game. This weakling of a guard was getting more confused by the second. It really wasn't fair for Ian to toy with him so much.

"Well, what package?" the guard insisted.

Och, if this were his guard at Balla Dorcha, Ian would have slapped him for being so dense. Then again, nothing ever happened at his holding on the Orkney Isles, which was why he'd spent so much damn time away from there, doing odd jobs like this one to feel a little blood running through his veins. A warrior like him was not meant to be wasted on an isle without a battle, which was why he crossed the sea to the mainland where conflict was rife.

"Ah, let me see. A lass. Tall, reddish-gold hair, blue eyes." He ticked off each of her qualities on his fingers.

Rhiannon's eyes started to widen beside the guard, and she inched away from her guard at such a slow pace the lad didn't seem to see her move.

"We've no one like that here," the guard said, and Rhiannon cleared her throat.

Ian could have laughed. "Lady Douglass sends her regards, my lady. I am Ian Sinclair."

Rhiannon laughed softly, the wicked glint in her eyes wiping away the caution she'd had there before. At least now she understood what was at stake here and wouldn't fight him in leaving this moron behind.

The dolt, however, finally picked up on the exchange and held his arm out in front of Rhiannon, his eyes desperately glancing back and forth between them. It was painful how slowly his mind seemed to be working. "Oh, no, you heathen, you'll not be taking his lordship's sister."

"It's quite all right, sir," Rhiannon said, pushing away the guard's arm, which moved a little too easily as she did so. "I'm happy to go." She started to edge to the right around the guard, her cat following, but the lad pulled out his sword in a show of eager bravado and leaped in front of her, waving it toward Ian.

In other circumstances that might have been as good as signing a death warrant. However, Ian preferred not to be the executioner today.

"Now, what are ye going to do with that?" Ian asked, pretending he was addressing a bairn who wished to be a warrior.

The guard thrust forward, and Ian easily dodged, not even bothering to pull out his own sword.

"None of that, lad," Ian said. "Put your sword away, and I'll let ye live."

"What?" the guard sputtered, still waving the sword around as if it were a bug catcher, not a flesh-slicing weapon.

"Let me live? You've not even got a weapon drawn. I have the upper hand."

"Now see, that is where ye're wrong, lad. I have no need to pull a weapon. I can beat ye bare-handed."

"Why, you insolent savage." The guard was growing rather purple in the face now.

Ian rolled his eyes at how worked up the wee lad was getting. Though he supposed wee wasn't charitable. He was easily in his mid-twenties and fully grown of body. Just not his mind. The efforts he was making were really pathetic, and also unfair Ian supposed. Plus, the longer Ian toyed with him, the less time he had to get Rhiannon out before anyone at the castle noticed she was gone. Or they were marched by on rounds, though as he'd observed yesterday, no one was doing many rounds anyway.

"Shall I put ye out of your misery, pup?"

That made the guard sputter and lunge, and all it took was a sidestep and a hard hit to the back of the unfortunate sap's neck to knock him out.

Ian nudged his prone body gently with his boot to make sure he was well and truly unconscious. When he didn't move, Ian glanced up at Rhiannon and, with a raised brow, said, "Well, now that that's done, shall we?"

A slightly horrified look graced her pretty face. That was another thing Douglass hadn't mentioned, how fair her cousin was. Not that Ian needed to pay attention to such things—he wasn't after a woman, just an adventure.

"You didn't kill him, did you?" she asked.

"Nay. He's merely asleep for now, but he'll wake soon and alert the rest of the castle. We'll need to get going—unless ye want to wait for your brother's arrival. And then more fighting and the chance that I am no longer able to bring ye to Scotland?"

Rhiannon's eyes widened, and she shook her head. "Oh,

no. I'm ready. I think." Her gaze turned skeptical. "How do I know Douglass sent you?"

Ian stared at her, confused. "I just told ye she did."

"That is true, but how do I know you're not lying?"

His brow narrowed. "Why would I lie about such a thing?"

"To get me to go with you." She said it as if it made all the logical sense in the world. And perhaps it did. But he suspected few Highlanders were walking into England saying that her cousin Douglass had sent them.

"And ye think I'd have come all the way from the Highlands of Scotland to this godforsaken land full of idiots just to snare one lass? That I'd have caught a wee kitten as a show of good faith for anyone?" As beautiful as she was, he didn't know anyone willing to come this far into the country alone for that. Scotland was full of beauties.

Rhiannon shrugged, then knelt daintily beside the felled knight, poking him in the shoulder. The lad didn't budge. She put a finger under his nose as if checking for his breath and seemed satisfied that he was still alive. Her cat followed suit, with a bat of her paws at the guard's slack chin.

Still no movement.

"Are ye trying to wake him?" Ian asked. "I'll just knock him out again."

"Oh, no, of course not." She grabbed a dagger from the guard's belt and stood.

"And what do ye plan to do with that?" Ian crossed his arms over his chest. This easy retrieval and retreat was turning out to be a little more tiresome than he'd imagined. He'd been having fun a moment ago, but he didn't want to knock the lass out to depart. Tossing her over his shoulder wouldn't be difficult, but it would slow his pace.

"For protection." She jutted her chin forward, flashing him a challenging look.

"Protection? From whom?"

"From anyone." She shrugged her dainty shoulders.

"I'll keep ye safe from everyone." It was his job, after all. If he returned to Scotland with any part of the lass harmed, Douglass would kill him. And then his brother would double-kill him for having to console his wife.

"Including yourself?" Rhiannon gave him a look that said she wasn't so sure.

Och, the lass was proving to be a challenge and insulting to boot. "I am an honorable man."

"I don't know that."

Ian rolled his eyes. "Ye will. Take the blade if it makes ye feel better, but I assure ye, ye'll not have need of it with me."

Lady Rhiannon threaded the blade through the belt at her hips and smiled at him in a way that was jarring in its radiance. "Excellent. Then, shall we?"

"Aye." Ian held out his hand, and she stared at it as if he were offering her a handful of ocean-floor scum.

"I don't think we need to hold hands," she said.

Ian grunted. "I thought it a better option than me holding onto your arm."

She squared her shoulders. "I prefer to walk without assistance. And I insist that Goosie come with us. Let us not argue the point—as you said, we need to leave quickly."

My God, she might be more stubborn than his brother's wife. And bossy seemed quite a tame description now that he had known her more than thirty seconds.

"Fine. But I'll not wait around for the cat if she decides to wander off. And ye canna fall behind, nor get too far ahead. Walk beside me at all times. Otherwise, I will toss ye over my shoulder and continue despite your protestations."

"Are we walking all the way to Scotland?" She wrinkled her brow in protest.

"Fock no." Ian grimaced. He'd not meant to say that. Too harsh for a lady's ears, but to his relief, Rhiannon laughed.

"Thank goodness."

"I have got a horse up the way." He'd left George not too far away as he snuck toward the castle to observe.

"How did you know I'd be walking today? It's been weeks since my brother let me out."

Weeks? Ian knew she was in a desperate situation. Something about being married off to pay a debt but let out? That sounded more as if she'd been held prisoner. As a brother himself, he couldn't imagine locking his sisters away. And quite frankly, if Rhiannon was anything like his sisters, like her cousin, it was lucky her brother was still alive.

"I didna know, lass."

"Oh." She seemed surprised. Her pace faltered a moment and then picked up again beside him. "Then how did you happen upon me?"

"I'd been scouting a couple of days and was trying to figure out which window to climb into." Her brother was most assuredly not good at protecting what was his. The guards weren't on a regular schedule, and sometimes posts weren't manned. Anyone could breach their fortifications with a little thought and observation.

"You think you could have breached the walls?"

"I didna think, lass. I knew." His plan had been simple, and he would have executed it perfectly if he hadn't happened upon her. She just seemed to make his day easier. The heavens might have intervened on his behalf.

"Oh." She was silent for a moment. "Is that why you said it was your lucky day?"

"Precisely."

She giggled. "It all makes sense now. I'm so glad you came. I didn't know if any of my letters even made it passed the castle walls."

"Letters? Douglass only received one." Ian frowned.

"Then it's a good thing I sent three."

But Ian didn't think it was good at all. That meant two hadn't made it to Douglass, and there was a chance at least one of them had ended up in the wrong hands.

Beside Rhiannon, whose boots clomped through the forest, Goosie's bell jangled. The noise mingled, sounding like freedom.

However, they hadn't made it very far before the massive Highlander bent down and gripped her cat's back with the same strong hands that had been prepared to grip her arm should she not come with him willingly, she supposed.

Sinclair brandished a mean-looking dagger, and Rhiannon gasped.

Immediately, she flew into action, slapping his shoulder, and his face. How could he have tricked her into going deeper into the woods only to kill her most precious pet?

"You will not kill my Goosie! I promised to go with you, and you said you weren't a devil but a rescuer, so what are you doing?" Each word was punctuated by a blow from her.

The Highlander growled. "Saints, stop it, woman. I'm no' going to kill your wee kitty. I'm merely removing the bell. Half the damned forest can hear us coming with the jangling. And the wee thing is likely starving, and having this damned bell sets off a warning to her prey before she gets even a chance to sink in her claws."

His words wounded as she took note of poor Goosie's thinning ribcage. Normally, in the castle, she'd provided meals daily for her cat, and she hadn't even thought of the bell when she'd assumed Goosie could survive until her brother let her out. After all, the stable was rife with mice for the taking.

"Oh, no." Tears welled in her eyes, and she picked up her cat, sobbing into her soft fur while her rescuer cut off the bell. He tossed it to the ground. "Oh, Goosie, do forgive me, you poor, sweet thing."

"She's free now. No need to sob. She'll be fine, and besides, all that noise will surely draw your brother and his cronies out of hiding."

Rhiannon shook her head, swiping at the tears. "They aren't likely to be hiding in the woods. Or anywhere, really."

"Shocking." He rolled his eyes as he said it and she couldn't help but laugh. "I had noticed their lack of attention and order."

Goosie squirmed in her arms, and she let her go, watching her leap to the ground and stretch before taking off.

"Oh," Rhiannon said, starting to chase after her. "She'll be lost."

"Nay, I doubt it. Animals have good instincts for finding their humans. She's got a nose on her, and as soon as she's run off her freedom, perhaps caught a mouse or two, she'll follow."

Rhiannon nodded, though she wasn't entirely sure she believed it. Goosie was also stubborn and sometimes remained away for days at a time. If she decided to do that now and they were far away on horseback, then how would she ever catch up? What if the cat forgot that Rhiannon wasn't at the castle and went back there? Oh, goodness, but her brother would likely torture Goosie until a miracle happened, and she figured out how to confess to Rhiannon's whereabouts.

Ian took hold of Rhiannon's hand, his grip sure but not forceful, and because she wasn't sure if she trusted herself not to run after Goosie, she allowed him to hold on. His stride was easily twice as long as hers, but she didn't want to complain. Already, he'd done much for her by braving the border crossing to rescue her from her prison. She had to trust that Goosie would follow; there was no other thought process she could cling to because anything else was miserable.

But after several minutes, she was panting and had tripped over a root, stumbling forward. Sinclair finally slowed, his narrowed gaze on her as if she had two left feet. And to be fair, she felt that way herself. Her toes were starting to go a little numb, and while she'd worried before about not bringing a cloak with her, she was hot and sweaty enough now not to have needed one.

"Are ye all right there, lass?" His gaze scanned the length of her, perhaps trying to discern if her legs worked properly, which she wasn't certain at this point.

"I'm tired." Who knew that being locked away for two weeks could weaken a person so much?

"We've barely walked a half mile."

"I've been running the entire time," she panted, rubbing a stitch in her ribs that stung. "And I've been locked in my room for two weeks. Have you ever been locked away for two weeks? Not much room for exercise."

"I have." The way he said it made it sound as if, indeed, there was room for exercise, and she'd failed.

But also, his being locked away was something she would need to question him on later. "Then you know what it does to a body. How it weakens you."

The muscles in the sides of his jaw flexed. "Indeed, I do, lass. I'll slow down. Or if ye prefer, I can carry ye. We've only another half mile until we reach my horse. Do ye think ye can make it?"

Not horses. Just *horse*. She didn't want to question him on that, fearing that he meant for them to ride together atop one horse all the way back to Scotland. Such close proximity made her skin tingle and her face grow flush. She was already having a tough time breathing; she didn't need to add panic to the mix.

"I can walk," she said, forcing herself forward. One foot in front of the other, that's all it would take. *One, two, one-two.* "Or run." If she had to, she supposed. Run as if Adam were on her tail—that seemed like good motivation.

"Good." Ian took her at her word and started to run, which put her into a full-out sprint, her skirts tangling in her legs, making it even more of a challenge.

The last time she'd forced her legs to move in such quick succession, she might have been eight or nine years old. That was well over a decade ago. Her muscles were not pleased with the exertion, painful even as sweat trickled down her spine, and she knew she'd be sore later, but there was no other choice. Even if she stopped, by the grip Sinclair had on her, he'd end up dragging her through the woods. She couldn't have him toss her over his shoulder and carry her to his horse through the forest as if she were nothing more than a bag of grain or a sack of wool.

She was a woman. A strong one at that. Give her a dagger, and she'd spear any foe's heart. Give her another week or two, and she'd be able to run the distance without suffering too much.

But as the seconds ticked slowly into minutes, which felt infinite, her aching feet and sore calf and thigh muscles begged for her to stop running beside him. To give in and let him toss her up on the hard round of his shoulder. To pass out and let her brother's men take her. She wheezed her breaths, sweat not just trickling down her spine but washing down her face as though a waterfall had suddenly sprouted near the top of her head. Every breath felt as if her lungs were going to explode. My God...she might die.

This was torture. And he must know it. How could her rescuer not hear the labored breathing that surely sounded as if she were about to keel over? If she'd heard someone huffing like that, she'd think they were close to death for certain.

When she was about to give up and collapse, the trees parted to the loveliest sight. A horse munching on grass, who glanced up from his green feast to see them, looking almost bored and as if he might say, "Took you long enough."

There was evidence of a camp having been made in the area, but Sinclair had made an effort to clean it up from the looks of things.

"Thank the heavens." Rhiannon's feet ceased movement, and she yanked her hand from Ian's to rest it against her knee, her other hand balancing on the opposite leg, bent over as she attempted to catch her breath and not collapse face first on the ground.

"Are ye all right?" Ian's voice was so full of concern it startled her.

Rhiannon managed enough energy to glance up and see his expression, which pretty much stated he thought she was addled.

Rhiannon sucked in a lung full of air and wheezed out, "Aye. Perfectly." At least she would be as soon as she had a moment to rest. Too bad there wasn't time for a quick nap. The grass looked soft and comforting.

Sinclair stared at her a moment longer as if trying to assess whether or not she was lying and then shrugged as he did, in fact, pick her up. Large, strong, capable hands wrapped around her waist. Rhiannon didn't even argue—what for? She didn't have the energy to pick herself up yet. Her legs were about to give out, and she didn't think she could walk another step even if he held a dagger to her throat. So, this one time, she would allow it and let him take the weight of her body off of herself and into his efficient hands.

Ian tossed her unceremoniously onto the horse, and she welcomed the coolness of the saddle against her heated muscles. Though the coolness lasted only half a second before it was replaced by the heat of Ian's body in the saddle in front of her.

"Hold on," he ordered, and she didn't argue, wrapping her arms around his waist.

As soon as she did, she regretted touching him intimately. Her hands settled on the muscular ridges of his abdomen, surprised by how hard he was beneath her palm, a marked difference from her own body. The heat of his skin practically singed her even though he wore a shirt of thin linen.

She'd never touched a man like this. Never sat with her legs pressed against a man's body. Her shins were on the backs of his calves. Her thighs were around his hips. Her breasts were crushed to his back.

Ian let out a slow whistle that she expected to be a signal to his horse, but instead, there was a rustling in the bushes, and a black ball of fur darted toward them.

"Goosie," she breathed, relieved her cat had followed them.

Goosie let out a little meow and then jumped into Ian's lap, content to sit on top of the horse, comfortable with Ian in a way that made Rhiannon smile.

The fact that her cat was trained to jump into a saddle on a rider's lap was her doing, as she'd often taken her cat for rides before her brother had come to Appleby Castle and taken her back to their family holding at Dacre.

From a distance, a great howl caused the hair on the back of Rhiannon's neck to rise. A bellow shuddered the air, and Rhiannon expected to see a demon rush through the forest.

"Your wee guard has woken," Ian said with a derisive chuckle. "His bellow will alert the others, and they'll see him running and send reinforcements. Time for us to go."

Rhiannon held tighter to Sinclair's abdomen with one hand, her other giving Goosie a little pat. Then Sinclair took off at a gallop, and she held on tight for dear life. Her cat curled up on Ian's lap as if runs like this made her nap. And at the speed they were going, Rhiannon laid her head against Ian's back, prepared to nap as well. Better than worrying about the guard and her brother's men following them. The ground flew by at such speed that she was bound to get dizzy if she kept looking too hard. So, she closed her eyes, refusing to let herself get sick from motion.

It was bad enough that Ian thought her weak and unable to run. If she lost her breakfast on his back, he'd likely make her run beside the charging horse. That would be a nightmare.

They sailed over the grounds, and though her eyes were closed, she kept her ears keen to any sounds of an approaching army. There was nothing but the steady rhythm of Ian's horse galloping through the forest and the beating of her heart, the rhythm of his breathing against her ears, and was that the faintest beat of his heart too? While hers pounded against her ribs, his was a sturdy rhythm, as if the run, the gallop, the being chased by armed men were nothing but a typical day for him. Nothing to worry over at all.

That was rather intriguing. She wasn't sure if she was irritated by the ease with which he seemed to move, to live, or if she was terrified that he didn't seem to care about an approaching army of men. He was only one man, and it didn't seem daunting to him at all that he'd be surrounded by at least a dozen guards.

She wanted to ask, but her words would be lost in the wind that funneled through her hair, and besides, at the speed they were going, she didn't want to distract him with silly questions. One wrong move on his part, and it would mean their death.

At least a half hour went by, before Ian stilled his horse after crossing a wide creek, the cool water licking the edges of her skirt and the tips of her boots. She glanced up and down the winding, shallow water, half expecting to see an army down the length pointing at them and issuing a charge.

Ian dismounted with Goosie leaping down to chase something. Ian reached for Rhiannon, and considering her legs were numb, she allowed him to put his hands around her waist once more and lift her into the air. As soon as her feet touched the ground, she wobbled unsteadily. Ian held her upright, and she was grateful for his attentiveness. Tingles prickled her muscles as they started to return to life. And finally, she told him he could let go.

"Why have we stopped?" she asked.

"Canna run poor George into the ground. He's a damned fine horse but not a god." Ian winked, the expression teasing and enticing all at once.

Rhiannon laughed to cover up how he made her feel—out of body, out of sorts. "No mystical creatures for you? I'm shocked."

"George thinks he's a unicorn, but he's just a horse with a lot of energy."

"He's beautiful." Rhiannon stroked her hand over George's soft neck, the hair of his mane tickling the back of her hand.

Ian grunted. "Take care of any business ye need." He

pointed to a tree that was barely wider than her leg. "I willna look."

"That'd be awkward for us both," she said with a little snort before taking off to find a bigger tree.

❧ 4 ❧

Ian stared after the retreating figure of his charge. Wild red-gold hair that reached down to hypnotic swaying hips. He had to force himself to look up, tantalized not only by her beauty but by the feistiness of her personality. Rhiannon wasn't a woman who took direction—and he admired that. He admired a lot about her—including her delicious backside. However, to keep staring was highly unfair, given there was nothing he could or would do about his unexpected desire for her. He'd been brought down by a woman before and didn't intend for that to happen ever again.

It wasn't even a great love. Not really even love at all. A woman he liked, a woman he'd lusted after. And when his defenses were down, she'd duped him. Led him right into an enemy's trap which had kept him locked up in a dank dungeon for nearly a fortnight before he'd managed to escape. Ian didn't harbor resentments. Doing so wouldn't help anything. But, he had learned his lesson. He was a man who looked to the future rather than ruminating on the past.

When Ian had finished his business, and George had

some water, he gave him little nibble of oats from his hand, waiting for Rhiannon's return.

There was a slight limp in her step as she approached, and he realized that she must have been overly exerted from their run earlier. Surprising that she would lack stamina. He knew from gripping her arm that she was not a weak woman. She had well-formed, if not petite, upper body muscles and even her waist had been trim but tight. Undoubtedly, she had some strength about her. Though perhaps her strength was not the kind gained by running.

The lass flashed him a grim smile as she placed one foot before the other. He could tell by the tightness of her eyes she was in pain, though she tried to placate him with the subtle curve of her upturned mouth.

But Ian wasn't the type of man to ignore a problem when it looked him in the eye. "Are ye all right, lass?"

"Perfectly." The word was spoken tightly with a clear "do not ask me anything else" edge.

Again, he didn't ignore her. "I do apologize for the...uncivilized way we're traveling."

"Uncivilized?" She picked up her cat and nuzzled its neck while the animal purred against her, equally pleased to be reunited.

"One horse, all the running."

"Oh." She waved his concern away dismissively as if the worry were a fly over her soup, though he wasn't too obtuse to miss the apprehension in her eyes.

"Once we cross the border, I've got another horse waiting for ye at an inn. The rest of our journey will proceed with more comfort. 'Twas just now, to escape from Dacre, a single horse was necessary."

Some of the worry faded then, and he could tell she was relieved. Though he'd enjoyed the feel of her riding behind him, he could also understand why a woman would not be impressed by having herself in that position.

"Well, that will be nice. Won't it, Goosie?" She tickled the cat's chin.

Ian watched their interaction with interest, only mildly jealous of the attention. Not that he wanted to be tickled on the chin, but watching how she cared for the wee creature made him realize how nice it must be to have such attention. And wouldn't that be nice if someone centered their attention on him? *Nay! Mo chreach...*

Ian turned back to George, trying to distract himself. "Why is your cat's name Goosie?"

Rhiannon let out a soft chuckle. "When I first found her, she was nothing more than six or seven weeks old. A wee kitten, but with the heart of a lion. She was chasing geese, meowing at them with this tiny, fierce howl. I fell instantly in love, and the geese rushed off, unwilling to be harmed by the miniature cretin." She laughed, the nostalgia of memory flashing over her features. "I took her into the castle and gave her some milk, and we've been thick as thieves ever since."

"Does she still have a hatred for geese?" Ian imagined how Goosie would get on at Buanaiche, where Douglass and Noah lived, and the geese who resided on the loch, the seagulls who dove for fish by the sea. Plenty of waterfowl and seabirds to chase.

"Very much so. They are her worst enemies." She gave Goosie one last cuddle before the cat gaped out of her arms in search of a prize in the brush.

"She is lucky to have found ye, lass."

"I think it is the opposite. I am lucky to have found her." The happiness that had dominated her features a moment ago wilted into sadness. "Especially since everyone I love is gone."

The emotion in her tone hit Ian like a stone. "Ye'll soon be reunited with your cousin."

She nodded, her lips turned down, and he wondered if she thought there was a possibility that he would not be able to fulfill his duty. "I do hope so. I miss her terribly."

"I am positive of the fact." And he needed her to be too. There was strength in believing in outcomes.

Rhiannon studied him, her gaze roving over his body in a way that was part observation, part judgment. "You think highly of your skills."

"I do. My brother would not have sent me if he thought otherwise. Ye can trust me, lass."

She cocked her head to the side, curiosity flickering in her gaze. "Your brother?"

"Aye, your cousin's husband is my brother. Did I no' mention that before?"

"This whole day has been so chaotic, I cannot remember. But I think it safe to say you have a personal stake in my rescue then so as not to disappoint your kin." For a second, he would have sworn he saw disappointment wash over her features before it was gone and replaced by a mask he was starting to recognize.

"Aye. And I care about your cousin." He looked at her pointedly, wanting her to understand this wasn't just any rescue mission, but family helping family. "The entire clan adores her, including myself. She makes my brother verra happy."

Rhiannon nodded, picked at something on the front of her gown and asked, "And does he do the same for her?"

Ian could read into the way she asked such an important question so casually. All she would have had before now was her cousin's letters, which might have attested to the nature of their very loving relationship, but still, Rhiannon might have been concerned. Worried if Douglass had been coerced.

After all, Noah had plucked her from the doorstep of their enemy and declared her his bride. But despite their not-so-conventional start, Ian had never seen two people more in love.

"Aye. Verra much so, lass."

"They are both very lucky." Rhiannon looked toward where they'd come from, the corners of her eyes pinched. "My brother betrothed me to his enemy. Consigned me to a life of torment and told me it was my duty. Since when was it a sister's duty to pay for a brother's debts with her life?"

"'Tis no', lass. He is no' a good brother. Nor does it sound as if he is a good man."

Again, her gaze focused downward as she shook her head. "Nay, he is not."

"And we will have more than one army coming after us. His and your betrothed?"

She nodded, eyes on the way they'd come. Ian noticed a tremble in her hands as she pushed her hair back from her shoulders.

"Probably so," she said with a shrug. "Though since I was betrothed to pay a debt, perhaps that man will take my brother's head instead."

"Does that worry ye?"

"Aye and nay." She reached behind her head and began to plait her hair, fingers moving nimbly through the locks slightly tangled from the ride.

"Care to explain?"

"Not really." Again, the casual shrug that belied the deeper feelings she didn't share.

"Fair enough." Ian understood her desire to keep her thoughts to herself. He hoped she'd feel comfortable enough to tell him when she was ready. For now, he gestured to the horse. "Shall we?"

Rhiannon nodded and stepped up to George's saddle. She

placed the cat on the leather, where Goosie pawed the reins as if she were about to take over and issue the order to gallop away. With easy grace, Rhiannon lifted herself onto the back of the horse, her long leg swinging over the side, a flash of her boots visible beneath the hem of her voluminous skirts.

Ian wasn't surprised at the ease with which she was able to mount and handle the horse. After all, Douglass was an excellent rider as well. Perhaps that was another thing their uncle had taught them well. Though he was English, the lord had deemed that the two women would be accomplished in things that some men deemed masculine. Ian just admired a woman for her abilities.

"Are you coming? Or are you going to examine me until my brother or his enemies arrive?" She raised a challenging brow in his direction, breaking Ian's not-so-discreet stare.

But rather than be embarrassed at being caught staring, he chuckled, somehow at ease with her teasing and not at all caring that she'd caught him raking her with his gaze.

Ian mounted, this time behind her. The warmth of her back seeped into his already heated chest. The exertion of their earlier escape had been extensive, and a few minutes' rest barely cooled him down. Which meant it was likely not enough for his horse either. And her round arse against his groin... this was going to be a long and arduous ride. He settled his hands on her hips and shifted her forward an inch, so she was at least not touching him. Mostly.

They were hours from the border, and he couldn't risk stopping for longer until they'd left England and safely made it onto Scottish lands. Not that they were always safer there, depending on whose land they crossed. But at least with his own people, he could negotiate far better than if the English stopped him.

For now, they would need to stick to the woods, which meant their pace would be stunted. But he was not willing to risk the roads with Rhiannon in his care. It was one thing if it were just him, and he could be assured of a clear path, but to put her safety in jeopardy for the ease of passage wasn't worth it. English soldiers and scouts weren't the only people who prowled the roads. Outlaws were always ready to rob and beat a man, leaving him to rot in the middle of the road.

Thankfully, the border was a straight shot with no mountain crossings, and they should be able to cross into Scotland by nightfall. It had only taken him a couple of days from Alistair's holding to arrive in England and scout out the place, allowing his horse time to rest as well while he waited overnight. Though the pace was slower with Rhiannon, he didn't anticipate it being more than a few hours longer of a journey.

And so, they slowed as they made their way through the forest until the trees started to thin, and they found themselves at the edge of a vast clearing.

Ian stilled his horse, examining the open field for any signs of people—men in particular. Whether they were trained knights or farmers, they weren't likely to be too keen on seeing a Scottish warrior and an English lady. Though he wasn't wearing his kilt, his demeanor and stance seemed to alert the uppity English that he didn't belong. And while he found his fighting skills far superior to most men's, he wasn't exactly looking for a fight, nor did they have the time to draw attention to themselves and risk a delay.

"What do you hear?" Rhiannon asked, turning in the saddle to peer up at him.

"Nothing yet."

"Then why don't you go?"

"Doesna mean I willna hear anything." Just the whistle of a slight breeze. The usual scampering of a squirrel. The flap of a bird's wings. George's huff of annoyance that they'd stopped.

"How long will you listen?"

"Hard to do it with ye talking, lass."

"Oh." She made an apologetic face and pinched her lips with her fingers, her eyes teasing.

Annoyed with their banter, it would seem, Goosie jumped down and started to stalk into the clearing, head down, tail up, as if the cat sensed something hidden.

The grass was a foot or more long, swaying in the breeze. There were a few matted-down trails, mostly from deer, but that didn't mean other things didn't use the created paths to hide their footsteps. Ian himself had done just that on his way to the castle to leave as little trace of himself as possible.

The cat must have sensed some prey, and given he'd not brought enough provisions to feed the animal, he let her have a few minutes to pounce. But other than a few field mice, there was nothing else here. At least not yet.

"Want to refresh yourself?" Ian asked, giving Rhiannon time to rest from the saddle and his horse a respite without their weight on his back.

Rhiannon nodded, and before he could dismount to help her, she lifted her leg over the horse's neck and then slid down nimbly his side as if she'd done it a thousand times.

She walked toward the thick trunk of an oak tree covered in rooted vines and moss, and he watched until she disappeared, then dismounted to stretch and relieve himself.

There was a subtle thump and then prancing paws as Goosie returned, a mouse caught between her teeth and looking as proud as possible.

"Oh, Goosie, what have you got?" Rhiannon rounded the tree, her expression showing pride at her wee cat.

But her smile faltered at the same moment Ian's did.

The sound had been subtle but enough that they'd both heard it. A crack, as though a boot had stepped on a dried-out stick, snapping it in half. Whoever it was realized their mistake, and the woods went silent. Even the breeze, once waving gently on the grasses in the field, slowed down to a stop. The world seemed to come quickly to a quiet end.

Ian stared at Rhiannon, all of his senses alive as he listened, trying to place the exact location of the crack. But whoever it was didn't want to be heard or found out, remaining silent and hidden. Goosie moved to stand between George's two front hooves as if seeking shelter.

"We know ye're there," Ian called out as he reached for his wrist, slowly sliding the small dagger from its hidden holder. He could throw it faster than he might be able to lunge with his sword and stop the advance of their stalker before they had a chance to get close enough to strike.

Rhiannon slowly started crouching, sinking as if her legs were melting into the earth. She'd stashed the dagger she'd stolen off her flattened guard in her boot and likely thought to help him. He shook his head at her, not wanting her to tempt whoever stalked them, but she rolled her eyes at him as if to say, "Don't be a dolt," and returned to standing, her dagger in her surprisingly steady hand.

A rustle sounded to Ian's left, slight, nothing more than the faint whisper of a fabric on the trunk of a tree, but he was keen to it, having trained his whole life as a warrior.

What surprised him, however, was that Rhiannon also seemed to hear it, her gaze turning toward the same spot. Interesting. The sounds were subtle enough not to be picked up by someone not trained to hear. He'd have to ask her about that later.

"Come on out. We've no' got all day," Ian said, keeping his tone bored.

A second later, someone did present themselves from behind a tree, but it was not at all who Ian had expected.

A child.

"Please, sir, don't hurt me." The lad couldn't be more than

six or seven summers, staring up at them with watery blue eyes, his lower lip trembling. He held his hands up in the air in a show of surrender. The clothes on his back were torn and dirty. Like a wee urchin who lived off the fruits of the earth. "I'm lost."

"Oh, my." Rhiannon started to walk toward the lad, her features softening, but then, for a fraction of a second, something changed in her eyes. The softness hardened, and before Ian had a chance to react, she was moving. Her arm wrenched back, and the dagger in her hand flew through the air toward *his* head. Ian ducked, feeling the wind of her throw against his face and then the unmistakable sound of steel meeting flesh behind him.

A guttural moan.

The thump of a body.

The clang of a weapon dropping.

Ian whirled from where he'd dropped down into a crouch, dagger in hand, to see a rough-looking man felled on the forest floor a few feet away.

The child cried out, "Da!" and rushed over to Ian, beating him about the shoulders, neck and face as great sobs escaped his throat.

Rhiannon was there in two seconds, wrenching the distraught lad away, cooing words against his head as she held him tightly. Why was Ian the one to bear the beating for her deed? Perhaps the lad had missed her being the one to throw the dagger. Perhaps he'd been taught never to hit a woman.

Everything had happened so fast that Ian had trouble wrapping his head around the facts. The lad had been a decoy. While the lad distracted the two of them, the father had snuck up behind Ian, ready to axe him to death. Outlaws, obviously.

And Rhiannon...

Holy hell. The woman had launched her dagger at the

outlaw, hitting him in the shoulder, the force of which had slammed him backward—the power to do that was incredible. In his fall, the outlaw seemed to have tripped over a root, falling and hitting his head, which had knocked him unconscious. Blood from his head wound and a knife protruding from his shoulder were enough to have the lad believing his father had crossed to the other side.

The lad was wailing loud enough to wake the dead. Ian's heart went out to him, for to believe one's father was deceased was terrifying, especially for one so young, but the wound Rhiannon had delivered wasn't a killing one.

Either she'd missed or done that on purpose, not wanting to leave the lad to raise himself, even if his only other option was to be raised by this outlaw. If the latter were the case, Ian's respect for her doubled.

"Your da's going to wake," Rhiannon was saying. "I promise. You'll have to wait a wee bit. Where is your mama?"

"She's gone."

"And do you have a brother or sister?"

Ian searched the surrounding wood, fearful they were about to be swooped upon by said brother or sister.

"Nay. Just my uncles and cousins."

Even worse. A hoard of outlaws ready to pounce.

"All right then. Are they far from here?";

Ian didn't know what she was getting at, but he hoped to hell she wasn't about to promise they'd take him to them. That was a one-way directive to getting robbed and slaughtered, or beat up at the very least. Though he'd fight like hell, and it seemed she might have a few fighting tricks up her sleeve, he didn't possess the strength of ten men.

"Not too far."

"Well, perfect then. They will come to get you soon."

Ian breathed a sigh of relief at that. She wasn't planning on taking the lad. He shook the man's uninjured shoulder, trying to wake him. Though he didn't want to take the lad anywhere, he also didn't want to leave him unattended.

The man's eyes fluttered, and he groaned. Then his eyelids shot up nearly to his brows, and he sat upright, arms shooting out to fight. But Ian was faster, grabbing his arms in a vice-like grip and shoving him back down.

"Calm yourself," Ian growled. "Your lad needs ye, and I'll no' be wanting to take ye away from him permanently."

"Da!" the lad's cry seemed to break through the man's furious haze, and he glanced over Ian's shoulder to his son, rushing toward him. "You're awake and not dead."

"Not dead yet," the man grumbled, glancing sideways at Ian.

"No' by our hands," Ian said. Then he gripped the dagger protruding from the man's shoulder. "Hold your breath, man." And he yanked it out.

Surprisingly, the man only grunted a little while his bulging eyes reflected that he probably wanted to scream. Holding strong so as not to scare his lad. Ian respected that, even if he didn't respect what had gotten them into this situation to begin with.

"We'll be going now," Ian said, cleaning off the dagger on some moss before handing it back to Rhiannon. "Dinna follow us."

The man only glared at him.

"Don't stand either until we're out of sight," Rhiannon added. "Or I'll be forced to put this dagger in your other shoulder."

Ian raised his brows at her, surprised at her threat. Who was this woman? Certainly not the damsel he had thought she was.

"Shall we?" She indicated the horse.

"After ye, my lady."

She shrugged and climbed up, snapping her fingers to

Goosie, who'd finished her meal and leapt into Rhiannon's lap.

The man on the ground grumbled, holding a wad of torn fabric to his wound. His son, however, seemed oblivious and was picking up sticks and tossing them the same way Rhiannon had thrown her knife. That likely irritated his father, having his son idolize the people who'd maimed him.

"Be a good lad, and take care of your da," Ian said.

The lad dropped the stick and turned to his father. "Are you all right, Da?"

Ian didn't wait for the answer but leaped onto his horse and urged him into a gallop through the field. The child had warned them his uncles and cousins were close. They were likely very near an outlaw camp, and the last thing he needed was for them to be caught in the middle of it.

They'd not get out as lucky as they had now. Not by a long shot.

5

Rhiannon jolted awake to a loud crack of thunder that shuddered her bones, followed by Goosie screeching and clawing her way up Rhiannon's chest in painful scratches.

Ian's grip around her waist and the steady gait of George beneath her grounded her at least in where she was.

As she tried to calm her cat, she gazed at the blackening sky and wrinkled her brow. From the dark shades of the heavens and the ominous swirling clouds, they were in for a mighty storm. A gust of wind blew, sending a shiver up her spine. As if to prove her point, a streak of lightning lit the gloomy gray, and another clap of thunder startled Goosie, who leaped out of her arms to the ground below, darting off into the shadows in search of safety.

"Goosie," she called, wrenching forward in the saddle, ready to leap down herself though they were still moving.

"Dinna fash, lass. She'll find us." Ian's tone was calm, his hold solid.

Even still, all she could do was worry. It was dark, and Goosie didn't know where they were any more than she did.

Another gust of wind rustled up her skirts and through her hair, snapping her locks back into Ian's face. He sputtered against the onslaught of her unkempt mane as she tried to wrangle it back under control, her arms flailing and trying to catch the long strands that had come loose from her plait—as they were apt to do in almost all situations.

"Damn," Ian mumbled, and the edge to his tone caused her to look back and see his face was pointed toward the sky. "We'll no' make it over the border as I'd hoped. We need to find shelter before the storm gets too bad. We'll be drenched soon, and 'tis unsafe to ride in a storm."

"Will our enemies stop?" she asked, thinking they had both an outlaw camp and her brother's men looking for them in the woods. One false move and they were dead.

"Aye. They'll no' want to risk being wet for the journey and taking ill, nor injuring their horses on water-logged ground."

Rhiannon hoped that was the case. The outlaws lived off the land and survived the outdoors all year long unless they were able to lay claim to someone's home, she supposed. Or maybe if they were able to find a cave. She glanced around the thick woods, not spotting a single cave in sight. She glanced up at the tall trees, which looked like bent and twisted arms, wondering if the outlaws had made a home in the treetops.

Above her, raindrops splattered on leaves, a pitter-patter in the forest. A few droplets made their way through the foliage. One landed on her nose in an icy drop, slipping to the tip and off. Over and over, the droplets came. Not a torrential downpour yet, but it was coming.

As another rumble of thunder bellowed across the sky, this time even George flicked his ears in concern, his muscles rippling with warning beneath them.

Ian dismounted, whispering words to his horse she

couldn't make out as he stroked George's neck. Whatever magic Ian was weaving seemed to calm the animal, whose skin ceased rippling beneath her. On foot, Ian led them deeper into the wood, where the rain took a longer path through the thick leaves to land on their heads. Finding nowhere to seek shelter, Ian settled on a massive tree, thick with foliage, which had a hollowed-out bottom for them to at least keep their supplies dry.

"We'll have to huddle here for a wee bit."

Rhiannon agreed, dismounting and helping him store his saddlebags in the hollow so their supplies wouldn't be ruined. He took off his horse's saddle and told her she could use it as a seat. Then he unrolled the plaid blankets he carried with him. Rhiannon settled onto the saddle, the leather still warm from their ride, and stared around the hazy forest for any signs of Goosie. She was glad they'd removed the bell, but it also made it hard to hear if her cat was nearby. Her mind told her to trust her pet while her heart wanted to burst from worry. Goosie had come back more than once now. This was no different—though, she would be terrified in a storm.

"Put this over your head for protection. It will also keep you warm." Ian held out one of the unrolled blankets.

Rhiannon took the offer. The fabric was thick, and while not exactly soft, it wasn't rough either. She wrapped it around herself and over her head like a cloak, tucking her knees close to her chest. Warmth instantly encompassed her.

"Thank you. I hope it's a quick storm," she said.

But Ian didn't look hopeful as he stared toward the sky, which had completely hidden the midday sun behind angry clouds. The forest had gone from illuminated to dark in a matter of minutes. With his horse secure, Ian plopped beside her, the heat of his body washing over her legs, her arms, on that side.

Rhiannon resisted the urge to scoot closer to soak up

more of his warmth. The storm had lowered the temperature, and the missing sun chilled her to the bone. To distract herself, she scanned the forest for any signs of Goosie, who had likely found a similar spot in a hollowed-out tree to ride out the storm.

Too bad she wasn't small enough to fit into the carved-out space behind her, though part of it did protect her back.

"You and Noah," she said, referring to his brother who had married her cousin Douglass. "You share a birthday?"

"Aye, with our brother Alistair."

Triplets? She could hardly imagine three Ians. "A rare feat to have three babes born together. Even rarer for you and your brothers to survive, though I'm sure you already know that."

"Aye." He flashed a grin. "And rarer for our ma to have survived and birthed more bairns after."

Rhiannon gave a slight shake of her head, amazed. "She must have been a very strong woman."

"The strongest woman I've ever known." Ian's voice had turned sad.

And she felt that deep longing within herself for a mother. "I wish I'd known my own better. She died when I was very young."

"Losing them is never easy, but having memories has helped ease the pain. I'm sorry ye dinna have that."

Rhiannon tightened the blanket around her shoulders. Sadness made her colder than she had been a moment before. "I had hoped when my brother retrieved me from Appleby Castle that he and I might be able to bond over our shared loss, but he refused to talk about them. At least my uncle did share stories with me. And he was so good at telling stories that I was able to imagine my mother through his eyes."

"Douglass's father?"

"Aye." She nodded. "He is like a father to me."

"When was the last time ye saw him?"

"Not long ago, maybe a year or so. But it might have been forever if you'd not come when you did." Uncle would have certainly come to Dacre, but with her being locked up in the castle and her brother dead set on selling her to pay his debts, she may not have been there to be rescued.

"Is your brother a gambler?" Ian asked.

Rhiannon bit her lip. "Yes. To be honest, he's no brother of mine beyond blood. What kind of man would sell his sister to pay a debt?"

"No' a man." There was a somberness in his voice that felt as if he had reached out to squeeze her shoulder in a metaphorical show of support.

"Exactly." She frowned, recalling how, in childhood, whenever she caught a glimpse of him—though the occasion was rare—she was always surprised by how little interest he took in those around him, —especially her. "Adam only cares about Adam."

"'Tis a shame he's such an arse, especially to his sister."

Rhiannon let out a heavy sigh, hoping some of the emotional burden of her brother's negativity would float away. It did not work. "He was named for our father. But other than stories, I don't remember our father well either. I can say that he was beloved of his people, and my uncle respected him."

"And so, your brother fell verra far from the tree, it seems."

"Aye." Rhiannon grinned. "Verra." This word she used in his accent, a teasing lilt to her tone. That did work to shove off some of the emotional heaviness that had taken her chest hostage.

"Ye need to draw out the 'r' more, lass. Verr-rr-rr-a, verra." He repeated the word with a flourish, his hand moving before him in an inverted arc as if that would emphasize the pronunciation.

Rhiannon giggled and repeated the word twice with the same hand flourish. "Like that?"

Ian chuckled, bumping her shoulder with his own. "Aye, well done. Would ye like to learn some more? Perhaps a little Gaelic?"

"Aye, why not?" She straightened up, almost forgetting her missing cat and the uncomfortable chill of the storm. "Have you something better to do? Some place to go?"

Ian chuckled, the sound deep and reverberating. "I do believe we will be stuck here a while longer. What do ye think, George?"

The horse glanced over, his eyes sleepy, obviously taking advantage of the respite to doze.

"As do I," Rhiannon said in an impression of the horse.

"Is that what he sounds like?"

She laughed. "Mayhap. But let us not discuss George's language when it is yours that I aim to learn a few words in."

"Ah, then, a Gaelic lesson ye shall receive. But fair warning, I will expect more George interpretations along our journey."

Rhiannon crisscrossed her legs and shifted so she could lean back against the tree and see him better from this angle. "I am eager and prepared to learn, sir."

"Laird," he said.

"Laird," she repeated.

"Aye, I am Laird Sinclair, no' sir."

Rhiannon lowered her voice, mimicking him, "I am Laird Sinclair, no' a sir in sight here, my lady."

"*Plàigh.*"

Rhiannon repeated the word and frowned, focusing on his face. "What does it mean?"

Ian grinned at her, though there was something teasing in the pull of his lips. "Lovely."

"Ah, that is lovely." She smiled, filing away the word to remember for later and thinking how their word for lovely sounded an awful lot like "plague"—ironically, a not-so-lovely word with terrible disease and pain etched into the vowels. "Another."

"*A' buaireadh.*"

Rhiannon repeated the word several times with his prompts for emphasis on certain vowels until she had it right. "And the meaning for that?"

Ian chuckled slightly. "Fascinating."

"What is so funny?" She narrowed her eyes at him. What was *Laird* Sinclair up to?

"Funny is *èibhinn.*" He winked, and for a moment, she was lost in his gaze. The smiles and laughter, the wink, the proximity. For a split second, all of it made her forget where they were and why they were there together. She rather liked not knowing better than remembering.

"Are you laughing at me?" she asked.

"*A bheil thu a ' gàire orm,*" Ian said in a high-pitched voice.

"Was that your imitation of a woman? Of *me*?" She gasped in mock outrage.

When he started to laugh harder, she smacked his arm—which was far too muscled. Well, to be truthful, it was perfectly muscled, and she wanted to grab hold and squeeze. Instead, she returned to her irritation. Focused on that. If she'd not been wrapped up in his plaid and shivering from the cold, wet rain, she might have tossed it aside and stood up to give him a piece of her mind.

"I think you're mocking me." She crossed her arms over her chest and gave him a glare her nursemaid had issued often.

"I might be," he said with an exaggerated shrug. "'Tis true."

Suddenly, she found herself quite irritated. More so than she was a moment ago. He was teasing her, aye, but perhaps she wasn't in a teasing mood. Perhaps she'd been running for her life and still was and didn't deserve it. "Do you know what else is true?" Rhiannon asked, leaning forward to make certain their eyes were locked.

"What's that?" The teasing dropped from the curl of his lips.

"It is true that I don't tolerate insults well." She leaned back, pursing her lips as she studied him.

"Have I insulted ye?" He appeared genuinely concerned.

"I do believe you have insulted my intelligence and certainly attempted to accost my feelings."

"Accost your feelings?" Now he looked confused; she could see the questions flashing in his eyes.

"Aye, by teasing me."

"Och, lass, ye have the wrong of it." Ian shook his head once, twice. "I never tease."

Rhiannon rolled her eyes. "And you expect me to believe that after the conversation we've just had."

"I do."

"You are much less intelligent than I thought you were."

"Oh? Ye thought me intelligent before?" He batted his eyelashes and pressed a hand to his chest.

She wanted to burst out laughing. Ian was obviously trying to diffuse the situation. But she was stubborn and was going to hold on a few minutes longer.

"Nothing more than a fleeting thought," she said. "An opinion that was quickly proven false. Do not get a thick head about it."

"Do ye think my head thin now?" Ian pressed his lips together in an obvious attempt to keep from laughing.

Rhiannon let out a grown. "You are impossible."

"I assure ye, my lady, I am verra possible."

"Then I am impossible." This time, she did push to stand, but right as she did, a rustle in the brush ahead gave her pause.

"We have company," she said, pulling out the dagger from her boot where she'd returned it after their encounter with the outlaws earlier.

Ian tossed off his plaid blanket and stood. He maneuvered himself in front of her, which was damned annoying, and then drew his sword.

Neither of them spoke nor breathed. Waiting as the rustling grew louder and louder still.

Rhiannon's heart pounded; she feared whoever lurked would hear it and know exactly where to go. The darkness of the wood only made their visibility of whoever was about to sneak up on them zero.

A second later, a loud "mrarw" sounded, and Goosie jumped from the brush toward them, instantly putting their guard down.

"Oh, you silly cat," Rhiannon said, while Ian opted for something a little more colorful.

Rhiannon stuck out her tongue at Ian, then turned back to cooing at her cat. She re-sheathed her knife and bent to pick up Goosie. "Where were you hiding? Too scared to stay there? Well, you are a sight for sore eyes and more than welcome to ride out this storm with us."

But it wasn't just the cat rustling in the thicket. The very real sound of boots on the ground, of something hard and sharp hacking at the brush, sent a chill up Rhiannon's spine.

All the blood drained from her face, leaving her lips to tingle as she stared at Ian, fear clutching her heart. He held his fingers to his lips as he silently re-drew his sword.

A whistle sounded from somewhere far off in the

distance, and there was a curse from no more than a dozen paces beyond their little hideout from the rain. Footsteps retreated, an answering whistle, and then silence.

Still, Ian stood, sword raised and ready to blot out the life of anyone who dared come through.

The seconds ticked and ticked into minutes, and then, at last, he lowered his sword and faced her. "Time to go, lass. Wet or no."

6

Bloody hell.

Ian cursed over and over again in his head, and sometimes aloud, as he pushed his horse into a pace he wouldn't normally require with this kind of weather, but he had no choice. All he could do was pray George didn't catch his hoof on a lifted tree root or step into a foxhole.

With the pace they set, Rhiannon sat pillion, and he leaned over his loyal steed's neck and begged him not to break his own neck.

Between curses and prayers, he held tight to Goosie, nestled inside his shirt. Just beneath his hand was Rhiannon's, cool to the touch but not trembling.

There was no telling which of their enemies was nearly upon them, but there was also no doubt that they'd been found out. Another second or two and whoever had been behind that thicket would have burst through to find them and alert the rest of his party. Until they reached Scottish ground, and even then, Ian couldn't let his guard down again. No more games, no more teasing. This was a serious rescue mission.

As it was, whoever had been cutting through the thicket had likely followed their tracks and would alert their leader to them anyway. Ian had tried to be careful as they rode, but in the rising storm, he'd wrongly assumed their enemies would also seek shelter. The bastards would find where they'd been lurking in the tree hollow: their footprints, his horse's hoof prints and even that of the wee cat. The best Ian could do now was put as much distance, as fast as possible, between them and their pursuers.

Mud from the wet ground flicked up and hit him in the face with cold, stinging splatters. At least Rhiannon's face was pressed to his spine, where she would be saved from the muck's assault.

Given the need for speed, Ian had opted for the more dangerous road rather than trying to find their way through the woods. Again, not what he'd planned in their retreat from England, but when one was faced with death at the hands of multiple enemies, sometimes those precautions had to be torn up and tossed into the wind.

In this case, his precautions had been tossed toward a stab of lightning and burst into flames. Neither he nor Rhiannon knew who exactly it was that followed them, only that it was not someone they cared to wait around and find out.

For her part, Rhiannon had not questioned him; rather she'd leaped to her feet and started to gather their things with a speed he hadn't expected from a lady. Unless, of course, it was his sisters or Douglass. And to be quite honest it was mostly rumors he'd heard. But Rhiannon continued to prove him wrong—save for the running, of course, which he was still puzzled over her lack of stamina.

She'd hustled them to depart quicker than a mama who'd caught her daughter flirting with the town lecher—and Ian was proud to claim he was not such.

Despite the violent nature of his pursuits, females considered him quite a gentleman. Though he'd had plenty of women in the Orkney Isles knocking down his door, ready and willing to let him do whatever he wished—all of which he'd declined. They brought gifts nearly hourly when he was in residence, batting their lashes in hopes of a favor or a wedding proposal, especially when he'd been named laird. It was part of the reason he'd taken off, leaving the safety of his lands and castle to his very capable second, Mac.

Ian longed for adventure. For the excitement of a challenge. He was more than happy to volunteer his body and sword to any cause—as long as that cause wasn't attached to a contract that ended with him saying "I do" for life and then being saddled to a woman who harped on him incessantly. And she would because he had plenty of faults.

Entering into marriage was not something he was willing to do. And why should he? He had two brothers. Sisters. If it came down to his life being forfeited and his property and title being up for grabs, he was more than happy for it all to go to them anyway—he had yet to confess to Rhiannon that he was the Earl of Orkney. He liked it better when she just thought him a simple laird. That made things less complicated for everyone.

Upon their father's death, his three holdings had been split between his sons with Ian granted the lands in Orkney, Noah the lands in Caithness and Alistair their holding in the lowlands. They were each also granted a title by King Alexander III before his death.

Noah and Alistair were far more capable of running estates and lands than he was. Ian was suited for adventure. Put him in charge of an army and a war anytime—even better if he was able to slaughter the invading *Sassenachs*, Rhiannon, her cousin and uncle excepted.

And adventure was what he lacked on the Orkney Isles. Certainly, he'd tried. There were festivals, monthly games.

Survival games—those were his favorite. They all went out into the woods and slowly but surely sought each other out, tagging each out of the game until there was only one survivor, the ultimate hero.

Of course, Ian won every time. But after the third time, he'd started to suspect they were making it easy for him because he was Earl of the Orkney Isles.

That wasn't helpful. He wanted to win in earnest. What good was victory when your opponent never picked up their sword? Ian wanted to sweat for his triumph.

How was he going to keep his skills honed if he was always allowed to win and no real threats ever came to their shores? No one seemed interested in the Orkney Isles. At least not in the last hundred years.

And thus, he'd decided to leave. Offering his services to his brothers, who had plenty of fights on the mainland between not only the English but local skirmishes as well. This was what he was good at. If he settled down with a wife and bairn on the Orkney Isles, wouldn't he get the adventure itch again? No woman deserved that.

Alas, he should count himself lucky that it was almost unheard of for his holdings to be attacked. His lands and people were safe. And he was immensely grateful to the gods and heavens and saints for seeing that they were. But, that left him an agitated beast who couldn't seem to satisfy an itch no matter what he did—until he'd left.

Ian maneuvered his horse on the muddy road with expert hands, avoiding deep puddles that hid rocks and cavernous ruts. He encouraged his mount to leap over fallen tree limbs that had come down in the storm. And at last, the familiar signs of the road leading into Scotland came into view.

"Foking finally," he mumbled, surging forward as a rush of relief flooded through his veins.

It wasn't as if Adam and his army wouldn't follow him

over the border; hell, Longshanks's men had done it a thousand times before in the Scots' War for Independence. The outlaws likely wouldn't, meaning they'd be safe from those bastards, since they did not want to tread on the turf of other outlaws, especially the Scots. However, the mercenaries—now they would blaze over the thick stones of Hadrian's Wall that lay between the two countries as if it were an invitation. Of that, he was certain. Because they'd been doing it for decades. An endless fight for power. For control.

More than once he'd found himself on the opposite side of the battlefield from a *Sassenach*, and he didn't doubt he'd find himself there again, this instance not included.

There was a border town, a few miles north of where they were now, with a tavern he'd stayed in many times. He built a friendship with the owner and his wife and helped whenever they needed it. They often hid him from his enemies, finding it a game of sorts, and he was fairly certain he could count on that now. Also, it didn't hurt that he compensated them well.

The skies still rained down, and the thunder and lightning had become so commonplace he barely noticed it anymore as flashes lit the path forward. Poor Goosie trembled in a tiny ball tucked into his shirt. The cat, too, would be relieved for the inn.

They blew into town, and he was forced to slow his horse. Though barely anyone was out in the storm, he didn't want to draw too much attention with his reckless speed. One never knew who exactly was in town, and though his friends wouldn't sell him out, it didn't mean that no one else would. While he would consider that person a traitor, he also understood that hunger and desperation did things to people. Made them make decisions they wouldn't otherwise have done. Made them turn on people, even loved ones, to ease the ache in their bellies. A few moments of reprieve from constant misery. Though he'd disagree with their decision, he could empathize with why they might choose that path.

They reached the inn, where the sign reading Thistle Tavern swayed violently in the wind. Ian eased his horse back to the stables, dismounting and leading George inside with Rhiannon still seated in the saddle, looking slightly perplexed but not openly questioning as she took in their surroundings.

He found it a little surprising she trusted him so easily, but then again, what choice did she have? And she trusted her cousin more than her brother, and he had been sent by her cousin to retrieve her. Still, Ian had not known her long enough to earn such blanket trust yet. A task he was determined to see completed—so he could feel pride in her dependence on him getting her where she needed to go.

But why should he care if she trusted him? After he dropped her off with Douglass and Noah, he would depart for his next adventure. See her whenever he saw his brother unless she married someone else in the clan. Then, he might not see her at all. Wives were often busy doing...whatever it was wives did. The thought of not seeing her made him ill at ease, he didn't know, and quite honestly, it made him a little nauseous.

Swallowing the bile rising in his throat at the odd turn of his thoughts, he cleared his throat until a lad no more than fourteen summers scurried from wherever he'd been napping.

"My laird," he said, swiping the rowdy pile of curls on his head out of his eyes and securing it with a leather thong. "Ye're back."

"Aye, lad." Ian tossed a coin, which the lad caught and tucked into the small pouch at his hip. "A bed for George, and take good care of him. He's gotten us from the hands of vengeful *Sassenachs*, and in a storm, no less. There's no such thing as spoiling him this night. Whatever he desires."

The lad nodded, his shoulders straightening at the idea of

being given such responsibility. "He'll be my number one charge, my laird, and I shall see to it that he is greatly rewarded for his services."

"I appreciate it. And so does he." Ian opened the loop of fabric over his chest to reveal Goosie. "Mind if this wee cat joins ye? She is a bit skittish, but good-tempered all the same."

"Oh, no," Rhiannon's tone was hurried and strained. She slid off the horse and came quickly to take Goosie from Ian's grasp, her cold fingers brushing his. "I'm afraid I can't part with her." She hugged the cat close.

Hearing her English accent, the lad's eyes widened, then he grinned at Ian. "I see why they were chasing ye. Ye're bonny, my lady."

Rhiannon smiled and said, "Thank you," while Ian resisted grabbing the lad by his ear and telling him to take back the compliment.

The woman didn't need to get a big head being called bonny, even if she was the most beautiful lass Ian had ever seen. And he refused to acknowledge that that wasn't the real reason he was irritated by the entire scene. Because he didn't want to think that she was bonny, and he damned well didn't want anyone else to think it either. And on top of that, he knew that a big head was the very last thing Rhiannon could ever possess.

Bloody hell.

"No' a word to anyone of our presence," Ian said, trying to change the subject in hopes he could stop staring at the way her plush mouth moved as she cooed to Goosie.

The lad nodded, serious again. "Ye have my word, laird, or ye can have my tongue."

Ian frowned. "I'll no' be going so harsh as that if ye squeal, but I may tan your hide."

The lad nodded, and Rhiannon gasped, shocked that he

would have suggested such a thing. Ian rolled his eyes and winked at the lad who knew very well Ian would never lay a hand on him.

Taking Rhiannon by the elbow, he led her into the back alley of the inn, cautious of anyone lurking. When he was certain they were not being watched or followed, he opened a door that had been cracked to let in cool air. Once through the door, they ended up in a warm kitchen that was surprisingly bustling, considering the weather.

The kitchen staff, recognizing him, only looked up for a second before they bent back down to chopping, stirring and serving. Their faces were slick with sweat as they toiled. And the results of that labor were savory smells that made his belly grumble. Clearly, a thick, hearty stew was in the burbling pots, and the scent of baking bread made him long to put his feet up at the nearest table and dive right into a hearty meal.

Alas, that wasn't going to happen until he had the lass safely tucked upstairs in a room, away from prying eyes.

As he met Rhiannon's gaze, he said quietly, "Wait here."

She nodded, tucking her cat even closer when Goosie tried to wriggle free. The last thing they needed was for the cat to make a disaster of the inn's kitchen. Ian ducked out of the roasting room, sweat already trickling down his spine from the humidity of the small cooking area. Immediately outside the kitchen, Ian slid behind the bar of the inn where his friend Gavin poured ale and slung jests to all the patrons at the bar. The sounds were jovial, hands slapping the soggy wooden bar top, shoulders bumping, and laughter crackling. Gavin's wife—along with a few other wenches, that he thought may also be a part of the family given their similar features—were rushing about the dining room, serving supper and mugs of ale.

"Ian!" Gavin caught sight of him, and a smile split his face, showing one missing tooth from a fight he'd broken up last year. He slammed down an empty pitcher and opened his arms. "My friend has returned."

"Gavin!" Ian grabbed the man in a mighty hug, and they tussled for a few seconds, bent over, trying to best one another, before Ian had him in a headlock. "An ale to let ye go."

Gavin mumbled through the hold, "Only if ye take me daughter to wife. Then ye can have all the ale ye want, son."

In accordance with their usual banter, Ian leapt back, hands up, shaking his head. "All right, all right. I'll pay. Your daughter, she is lovely, but I am spoken for."

Gavin chuckled and raised a skeptical brow. "Spoken for by the sword, more like. Didna think we'd see ye back here so soon."

"My retrieval didn't take nearly as long as I'd thought. And what's wrong with vowing to always be true to the sword?"

Gavin grinned, appreciating Ian's devotion. "Nothing. All the better for ye."

"Aye." Ian glanced around the tavern, noting a few familiar faces in the regulars and a few he didn't recognize. "I need a room. For my charge. And a meal sent up to her."

"A 'her?'" Gavin wiggled his brows. "Ye bastard. That talk about a sword, and ye had a wench all along."

Ian rolled his eyes. "'Tis no' like that. I need to keep her out of sight. We may or may no' have a few angry *Sassenachs* following us."

Gavin shook his head. "Bloody hell, man."

"I'll pay double. But I'll also respect your wishes if ye ask us to leave. I know 'tis a lot to ask of ye."

"I could never ask ye to pay double. Ye know we'd hide ye without the coin. Besides, I love a wee skirmish myself." He grinned wider, proud of his missing tooth.

"I dinna need to be hidden as none of them have seen me

yet. But the lass, I think she'd be safer tucked away. And I'll pay double all the same."

"If ye insist." Gavin nodded toward his wife, Sarah, and she scurried over, a pleasant smile on her face at seeing Ian. "Brought a woman with him."

"Oh," Sarah squealed, clapping and leaning around Ian to see where the mysterious woman was. "Is that so?"

"Nay, no' like that," Ian groaned. They'd have him wed before the hour was through. "She's a... Well, anyways, I'm her escort, I suppose. She and my brother's wife are cousins."

"Ah, well, perhaps 'tis best to keep it out of the family," she said. "Dinna need that kind of trouble. Where is she?"

"In the kitchen. I didna want to bring attention to her, as we're in a bit of trouble. *Sassenachs*," he whispered the latter.

"Ah, I see. We'll get ye both settled, not to worry." Sarah whirled around toward the kitchen with Gavin in tow.

In the kitchen, Goosie was weaving her way around all the staff's legs, and Rhiannon was giving the scullions a lesson on chopping.

"See, if you hold the onion like this, your fingers bent under like this," she demonstrated, with a mesmerizing speed and accuracy, "you won't have to worry about cutting yourself again."

Ian noted that one of the said choppers was holding a bloody rag on their finger, which was likely the impetus for this lesson.

"Now you try," Rhiannon instructed one of the other scullions, who was slow at first and then quickly gained speed. She turned again to the injured helper. "Once you get that finger bandaged up, you'll be back to chopping in no time and without any injuries."

"Oh, can we keep her?" Sarah asked, pouting up at Ian.

Ian chuckled, his gaze drawn back to the woman in question, who continued to impress him with each passing minute. "Only with her permission, though I think my brother and his wife might have my head if I leave her behind."

"Fair enough," Sarah conceded with an exaggerated sigh of disappointment.

"My lady." Regrettably, Ian interrupted the lesson. "When ye've finished, Sarah will take ye to your room."

Sarah wiggled her fingers at Rhiannon and thanked her for teaching the scullions a better way to chop. Rhiannon graced her with a smile that did something funny to his insides. She retrieved Goosie from where she'd been lapping at a small bowl of milk laid out for her by one of the kitchen servants.

"Oh, thank you so much," Rhiannon said. "Would it be too much trouble to take some of this delicious stew to my room?"

"None at all, dear, and if ye'd like a bath, too, I can have the tub and some hot water brought up."

"Oh, a bath? I would love one. I probably look a fright. So much mud outside. The storm and all."

"I dinna think ye could ever look a fright," Sarah said with a tut of her tongue.

Ian also didn't think it was possible for Rhiannon to look anything other than stunning, even with flecks of mud on her face and hair. In fact, he found the flecks of muck to be somewhat endearing, which likely meant he was deranged. Alas, he would have to live with that notion because as hard as he tried not to notice her, he was incapable.

Ian followed the two women upstairs, keeping an eye on anyone who happened to be watching them from the tavern below, part of which had a view of the stairs. One man in the corner booth looked to have drunk an entire barrel of ale and was therefore not a threat even if he tried, and then there were a few men who nudged each other that were drinking at the bar. No one else seemed to care, or at least didn't look long enough to give Ian pause. Good.

Sarah opened a door—third on the right from the stairs, Ian noted—and showed Rhiannon inside. There was a large bed, a brazier for a fire and a very small table with two chairs, along with a slim wardrobe that had seen better days from the looks of it. The room was small but cozy, and though the furniture was tattered from age, the space was clean and well-maintained.

"I'll be back with your supper and bath," Sarah said, eyeing Ian on her way out with a question.

He could tell she wanted to ask about his sleeping arrangements, which he'd not yet thought of, only that he knew he would not be sharing a room with Rhiannon. Riding a horse with her was temptation enough. Though for safety's sake, it was probably best for him to stay here with her. To protect her in case the English came and they had to make a hasty exit. Then again, his gaze trailed to the bed. There were a lot of things that could happen in a bed with a bonny lass, and he didn't want any of those ideas to come into his head.

Except it was too late for that now, wasn't it? He pictured of Rhiannon's red-gold hair spread out on the pillow, her lithe body naked and soft beneath his.

Ian cleared his throat and wrenched his gaze from the bed toward Rhiannon, only to see that her gaze, too, had been fixed on the mattress, and her cheeks were flaming red. Was it too much to imagine she was seeing the same thing he was? Och, the naughty lass.

She let go of Goosie, who quickly leapt onto the bed and curled between the two pillows. The proverbial douse to flames, except it only made Ian think that pillows had been laid there for two heads.

"I'll let ye have the bed, of course. I'll likely stay in the barn with George. Wouldna want my faithful mount to miss me for too long."

"Oh, I couldn't let you stay in the stables." Rhiannon flicked her gaze toward his, her lower lip drawn in between her teeth.

Dear God, he wanted to be that lip. Again, he found himself clearing his throat to knock some sense into himself, except the simple act did nothing to quell the heat in his blood. "I've done it many a night. Quite comfortable. Besides, it will help me keep an eye on everyone who rides through town. I'll hear anyone approach. At the first sign of trouble, I would rather be there so they dinna make it inside."

"Ah," was all she said, her gaze sliding back to the bed. This time, at least, she nodded, and he hoped that meant her thoughts had turned to sleep. "Thank you for today, for everything. I had no idea how I would get away from my brother. I prayed daily for the ability to escape, and you gave me that."

"Your cousin gave it to ye. I'd no' be here were it no' for Douglass's request." This was the truth, but he hated how it made it sound as if he hadn't wanted to take on this quest. All the same, perhaps it was best to put some distance between them.

Rhiannon looked him right in the eyes then. There was no wavering in her voice when she said, "She might have asked, but you didn't have to volunteer. You risked your life for me. And for that, I give you my thanks."

The way she stared at him, the intensity of her gaze—he'd never met a woman filled with such confidence, and it reminded him again how much she, unlike any other woman, had the power to captivate him. "And ye saved mine today, too," he said, referring to the outlaw in the wood. "We're even."

The corner of her mouth hitched into a slight smile. "I

supposed we may be even for now, but I have a feeling, given what we've run into thus far, we're bound to have a lot more trouble before we reach my cousin's castle."

He nodded. "That is likely true."

"Do you think we'll have trouble tonight?" She glanced toward the window, covered in a thick wool curtain to hide the outside from seeing in. Only the subtle wring of her hands showed that she might have been the slightest bit nervous, and he wished there were a way to comfort her, to assure her they wouldn't.

But the truth was, she was right. Every second that ticked by made it much more possible for their enemies to find them. He'd rushed to get here after they were discovered, and aye, the army hunting them wouldn't know the roads and villages as he did, but it was only a matter of time before they arrived here and banged on the tavern, stomped up the stairs and kicked in the chamber door. He hoped by the time that happened, the sun would have risen, and they'd be on their way, his coins in Gavin's hands not only for his silence but for the damage the *Sassenachs* were likely to leave in their wake.

"I hope that we dinna, my lady. But I canna make any promises. The world is a wild and unpredictable place."

"At least there's hope, even if it isn't guaranteed."

"Aye." He gave her a small smile. "I'll no' lie to ye, lass. But I will pray we are unbothered while here."

"I appreciate that." She reached for her boot, lifting the hem of her skirt as she did so, and Ian was momentarily without breath. Besides her boot, there wasn't much to see, only a hint of her hose. But still...it had him imagining she would lift it higher to show off her soft and delicate knee. Instead, Rhiannon pulled out the dagger he'd given her. "Can I keep this? For tonight?"

"Of course," he said, somewhat relieved because, for a

second, he thought she might have been considering gutting him for his inappropriate thoughts.

Ian reached into his sleeve and pulled out another, walking toward her. "And maybe this one too."

"One for each boot?"

"Actually." He slipped the daggers from the brace at his wrist, undid the fastener, knowing he had a spare in his satchel. "Here."

Ian held out his hand, silently asking her to put her hand in his. She did so, and he slowly peeled back her sleeve, revealing creamy, soft skin. Good God. He held his breath, afraid she would hear the sharp inhale and slap his hands away. Rhiannon sucked in a breath, the sound while subtle in reality was like thunder in his ears—the same inhale he'd tried to avoid. Gooseflesh rose on her skin where he touched her, and he worked hard to ignore the rush of blood winging through his veins in response.

He gently tightened the brace on her wrist so it wouldn't slide. "Just keep it in like this." He slid the dagger into place, the motion slow and sensual, which seemed at odds with the violence he hoped she'd wrought on any enemy who gave her cause to use it.

"Thank you," she whispered.

Ian glanced up at her. His hands were still on her wrist. Their eyes locked, and he found himself practically drowning in the depths of her sky-blue eyes. They were fringed with dark lashes, thick and curled. Mesmerizing. Honest.

He cleared his throat, trying to break the spell, but it didn't work. Let go of her, he told himself, but his grip remained steady, and she made no move to pull away. He sensed her coming closer. She licked her lips. Her gaze boldly roved down to his own lips where she stared for half a beat before glancing back into his eyes.

Ian had been around enough women to know what that

look meant. She wanted a kiss. And goddammit, he wanted to kiss her too. Wanted to press his mouth to hers and claim those subtle pink lips for at least thirty seconds and taste her. Plunge his tongue inside so he could say he knew what sweetness tasted like.

When was the last time he'd kissed a woman?

It had been years.

He wasn't one to bed women often, finding it distracted him from the adventures he sought, but also because he did not want to be entrapped. He was not the kind of man who would bed a woman and leave her with a child to deal with it alone. And he'd figured that out at a young enough age, making sure he didn't leave any bastards in his wake. The few women he'd slept with had been older—out of childbearing age. Or at least they'd told him that. And despite their claims, he still didn't take their word for it. Used extra precautions and did not finish inside them.

Thankfully, his father had taught them as lads that doing so might prevent a bairn. One of the many good lessons he'd taught Ian and his brothers. That lesson had been embarrassing, to say the least, considering his da had asked all three brothers if they'd ever wanked themselves off. But knowing what came with release—the seed that spawned a life—had been necessary to keep themselves from fathering a dozen bastards. So, however embarrassing it had been, Ian was grateful for the crude lesson.

And thinking about that made him finally let go of Rhiannon's hand. He cleared his throat again as he took a step back. God, if he kept this up, he might have cleared his throat right out of his neck.

"Well, lass. I do hope ye have a good night. I'll most likely see ye in the morn. Pray no' tonight."

Rhiannon blushed, realizing he'd rejected her, which only made him wish to sweep her into his arms and ask her to forgive him. To kiss her properly. To make them both see stars.

"Thank you, and a good night to you, too, my laird."

So formal. A good reminder of her relationship with him —ward and escort. Exactly what he needed.

"Lock your door, my lady," he instructed, returning the formal tone and regretting every damn syllable.

7

Rhiannon woke with a start from a dream where she'd been running through the woods, invisible men with axes chasing her. When she'd been about to run smack into a tree, she'd jolted awake, the sound of her body smacking the trunk still echoing in her ears.

She rubbed her eyes, her body slick with sweat.

There was the smack again. What was that noise?

She sat up in the darkened room. A sliver of moonlight cast through the window, illuminating the small chamber in murky shadows. From the heaviness of her eyes, she didn't think she'd been asleep long. Maybe an hour or two.

Goosie hissed from somewhere near the chamber door at the same time that the floorboards outside her rented room creaked. Rhiannon sucked in a breath, gooseflesh rising on her skin, suddenly very much awake.

If her cat was on high alert, that meant someone was approaching who shouldn't be there. Could be another guest. Her room wasn't the only one in the inn, but she couldn't shake the thudding sound that had woken her. Something wasn't right.

She tried to think, her mind picking apart the pieces of her recent memory, which was filled with dreams of Ian, nightmares of running through the woods from her brother, and at the tail end of it, a loud bang that had woken her.

There it was again. A thud so loud it felt as though it was rumbling the floor beneath her bed. Her fingers curled into the blankets as if holding tight to them might ground her.

She strained to listen. There was a bang now and then, as if someone had knocked into a chair and sent it crashing to the floor. Or maybe backed up into a table or tripped and fell.

The same sounds one might hear of a bar fight. Though lacking in shouts as she would have suspected.

A creak again outside her door. And even in the shadows now, she could see Goosie's back curving, tail up, ready to attack whoever came through. This was not someone passing by on the way to their rented quarters. This was someone lurking. And Goosie was an extraordinary cat who understood danger and was ready to fight for her mistress. Rhiannon wasn't going to leave her to be the only one defending this sanctuary.

She slipped out from beneath the covers, trying not to make a sound, her bare feet frozen against the floorboards. The dagger was still in its brace at her wrist, but the one she normally kept in her boot was on the nightstand beside the bed. She picked it up, prepared to hurl it at whoever came through the door.

Muffled voices. One deep, stern, the other belligerent. She couldn't make out the words, only a dull murmur through the door. A thud, then another. She realized those were the sounds of fists hitting flesh. Two men were fighting outside her door. She prayed one of them was Ian and that he was winning.

The door to her chamber shuddered as a body landed against it and then again. She held her breath, her body braced and ready to fight. As the men continued hitting the door, Goosie gave up on her bravado and hid under the bed. Rhiannon couldn't blame her. She, too, might wriggle her way under the mattress, close her eyes and will the nightmare away.

More scuffling. Sweat poured down her back; her hands were damp. "Oh, come on," she urged. "Come through the door. Let's get this over with."

This torment of "will they or won't they" was going to drive her mad. Mad enough that she might even open the door herself. Besides, if they took too long, she was liable to miss her mark with her slick hands, making it hard to grip the dagger for a proper through. Rhiannon rubbed dampened palms on her chemise—the only thing she'd had to sleep in given she'd not exactly packed for this trip—then resumed her stance.

If they didn't come through the door in the next thirty seconds, she was going to open it. The anticipation was too much. She'd be no good during a siege. Patience was not a virtue she possessed.

Deciding that she couldn't wait any longer to end this, she started to march toward the door when it shuddered again with a great bang and this time, the wood splintered. Had someone kicked it?

Hard to tell. But her fear renewed, sending her heart skittering to somewhere near her feet, and she backed away from the door, her muscles tense, her eyes scanning, ready to injure whoever came near her.

"Where are you, Ian?" she muttered, hoping it was indeed him on the other side of the door trying to fight off her would-be attackers.

Another crash as something slammed against the door, and then there was a foot poking through. She didn't hesitate. Rhiannon flung her dagger toward the foot, catching it in the middle. Only as it sunk into the sole of the man's foot did she think that perhaps she should have ascertained that it was not Ian's. Then again, if he was kicking in her door, that was a lesson he needed to learn. And unless something had changed in the few hours she'd been asleep, he would not be the one trying to break in.

The man yanked his foot loose of the splintered wood, bellowing his pain and anger.

Ian's face appeared in the hole where the foot had been. "Well done, lass." And then he disappeared again, the sounds of the scuffle quick as he put an end to her attacker, and silence reigned on the other side.

Ian reappeared in the hole. "Would ye mind opening the door, my lady?"

Rhiannon wanted to laugh with relief. At the same time, she wanted to be furious. Instead, she settled for a quiet huff and a large breath of relief as she hurried over and lifted the bar from where she'd placed it a few hours ago. Even with the damage, it was relatively easy to yank open the ruined door, though it creaked a little more on the hinges than she remembered.

"Who is he?" she asked, staring at the felled man outside her door.

Ian retrieved her dagger, cleaning it on the man's shirt before handing it back to her.

"No' a *Sassenach*, but I suspect they paid him off. Saw him sneaking around the back of the tavern." Ian entered the room, his hands on his hips, sweat on his face. "Are ye all right?"

"Aye. Perhaps I should ask you since I have saved you once again." This she said rather saucily, partly because it was true that she had now assisted him twice and partly because she was still a little embarrassed about what had happened last night.

The air between them had crackled. And the warmth of his solid hand on hers as he'd tied on the brace had done strange things to her. Made her want to melt into him. Thoughts of kissing had invaded her mind, and then she'd found herself leaning toward him. Wanting to see what it would feel like to be kissed by a man like him. To be swept up in that moment.

But Ian had backed away, putting a sizable distance between them, and spoken as if she were a stranger. So formal that it had rankled. And certainly squashed any desire for a kiss. She'd wanted to lash out, to shove him out of her rented chamber, because that would have been easier than facing his rejection. Alas, she'd managed to be as stoic as she could. Which, she believed, gave her the higher ground. And at least it made her not cringe.

But she wasn't going to hold back now. Oh, nay, she was ready and willing to give him hell if he deserved it.

Ian studied her, eyelids squinting as if trying to understand everything about her in one glance. A feat which she would never allow him to succeed at. His gaze roved up and down her nearly nude body in the moonlight. Her chemise was damp from the sweat of her dreams and then the sweat of her fear, clinging to her hips, her belly, and her breasts. The thin muslin stuck to her back and rear, which he fortunately could not see. However, there was a part of her that wanted him to see how the fabric molded to her heated skin. To witness what he was missing when he'd rejected her.

Heat blazed her cheeks at the wanton thoughts. Goodness, but why was she thinking like that? She was a lady. Though, when had she ever been proper?

Rhiannon wanted to kiss him still, despite his clear message the night before that he didn't have any interest. Then why was he looking at her like that now, his gaze lingering on the places that made her a woman? Perhaps it was because he, too, wanted to kiss her but had denied himself the pleasure given their circumstances.

The silence between them sizzled. She wasn't certain how long she could take it and if she could even move to break the spell—other than to close the distance between them, to press her body to his and end this torment.

Ian took a step closer. Then another, stopping again. There was still half a room between them. The air crackled with heat. All it would take was a few steps from them each to reach the other. Toe to toe. Knee to knee. Belly to belly. Face to face. And then lips to lips.

Rhiannon couldn't take her eyes off his face, watching the conflicting thoughts moving over his features. A wrinkled brow, heavily lidded eyes that roved, a mouth pressed together in firm determination, and jaw muscles flexed with indecision.

And at last, she was satisfied. He'd rejected her, but he wanted her. As much as she wanted him. Especially now, with the blood of fear and fighting rushing through her veins. There was a need for more excitement and release, and with how he looked at her, she knew instinctually what thrill both of them craved.

They felt desire. Potent and heavy.

Rhiannon wasn't experienced in the ways of the flesh, but she did know desire. She'd kissed a man before, not one her uncle had approved of. And it had been nearly eight years ago. She'd been seventeen. They'd had a festival, and as they danced around a raging bonfire, the son of a neighboring lord had taken her hand. They'd frolicked and flirted, and she'd had one too many cups of fruity mead. But not enough to make her mind fuzzy. Not enough to excuse having said yes when the young lord led her behind one of the tents and kissed her senseless. Not enough to deny his touch on her breasts, between her legs. And not enough to have not recognized his arousal as he pressed it against her hip.

They'd been about to fall to the ground and make a mistake when her uncle came upon them, fuming mad.

At first, she'd been mortified, and then she'd been grateful. Desire made her head go hazy, her morals evaporating with a single kiss. Made her say yes when she needed to say no.

Like right now. Every inch of her body hummed. A primal urge pushed her forward. Made her fingers itch to touch him and be touched. To let his mouth crash on hers and devour her whole.

But her uncle's voice in her head forced her feet to remain where they were. Danger lurked, and in one breathless moment, with their guard down, they could become easy targets. A dead man was outside the door, and lord knew how many more were downstairs. She couldn't rip off her chemise and beg Ian to make love to her. Though the idea was appealing.

Booted footsteps pounded on the stairs, breaking the spell between them both. She lifted her dagger, prepared to defend them again, and Ian drew his sword.

"Ian?" Thank goodness Gavin's voice broke through the thickness that was their fighting response. They lowered their weapons, his footsteps pausing outside the door. "Och, I see ye already had all the fun." The larger man stuck his head in the door and then quickly withdrew. "Pardon, my lady, I didna realize ye were indisposed."

Rhiannon groaned. "Oh, no, I am so sorry. There was no time to dress as that man put his boot through my door."

"I trust Ian is acting with chivalry?" That was the voice of Sarah, who must have come up behind her husband. "And by 'that man' ye mean this one out here."

"Aye, the still one. And, indeed, Ian is always decorous."

Rhiannon grabbed the blanket on her bed and wrapped it around herself. "I am covered."

Gavin and Sarah came in then, both of them looking worried and scanning the room as if more vagabonds might be hiding in the shadows.

"There will be more coming." Gavin's voice was steady, his gaze holding a hint of warning. "Word is they're offering quite a bounty on your head. Those who know ye willna dare to give ye up, but there are plenty who are hungry and dinna care."

"Understood." Ian reached into his sporran and tossed them a leather pouch. "For your troubles."

"We'd do it for free." Gavin caught the bag of coins and gave Ian a nod. "But it will help in the cleaning up."

"Until next time." Ian clamped his hand on the big man's shoulder, and they nodded in mutual respect.

"Might I get dressed before we leave?" Rhiannon stared down at the blanket wrapped around herself, feeling suddenly vulnerable. It would be quite difficult to run like this and not expose herself to strangers. "Is there time?"

"Oh, my goodness, aye. Ye men get out of here." Sarah shooed the men out as if they were children with dirty feet on a newly scrubbed floor and then shut the door behind them.

Ian poked his head through the hole, saying, "Meet me outside when ye're finished. And make haste."

"Oh, shoo!" Sarah said, rushing toward him, and Rhiannon laughed, feeling the woman might bash him on the head if he didn't leave. "Men." Sarah rolled her eyes and then opened the wardrobe to pull out Rhiannon's gown. She smacked and shook it, trying to shake off some of the dried dirt flecks.

"Thank you for your help," Rhiannon said.

"Oh, 'tis nothing. I do wish we'd had time to clean this for ye, though. That poor gown has seen better days."

"Nothing a little scrub can't remove." Rhiannon smiled and discarded the blanket. "I'm certain once I reach my cousin, I'll have it washed and mended good as new."

"Good. I take it ye were no' able to pack anything."

"It was go or stay and nothing in between."

"Ah, I understand. Want me to give ye a few things just in case?"

"I couldn't."

"Ye can, I'm offering. Willna take me long. At least another pair of hose and a chemise."

"I'd appreciate it."

"My pleasure." Sarah helped her into her gown and then left to gather supplies while Rhiannon finished getting herself ready.

She got down on her hands and knees, poking her head under the bed in search of Goosie. "Come out, come out, wherever you are."

Goosie let out a mournful meow as if she'd been traumatized by the whole ordeal.

"Oh, you poor thing. Come now, and let us get you out of this place." Rhiannon wiggled her fingers, hoping to entice her cat.

Goosie approached her cautiously and, sensing there was no further danger, rushed into Rhiannon's waiting arms.

They descended the stairs to find Sarah with a small satchel waiting at the base. Though Sarah tried to block the mess of the initial fight from view, the woman wasn't large enough to do so, and Rhiannon could see a few more downed bodies and overturned furniture.

"Here ye are, my dear," Sarah said, loud enough to snap Rhiannon's gaze back to her. "No need to worry about returning a thing. They are yours to keep."

Rhiannon hugged the petite woman, wishing she could have stayed longer, at least to have helped clean up the mess.

"Consider it payment for helping my poor cooks in keeping their fingers out of the way of their knives." Sarah grinned at her.

"I would have done that for free." And she genuinely would have. Rhiannon loved to help others.

"Aye, I know it. But who doesna like a second pair of hose on a long journey?"

"I suspect no one." Rhiannon giggled, clutching the prized pack of extra hose.

"Well, ye'd best make haste." Sarah shooed her along. "There's liable to be more trouble ahead for ye, and I dinna want to be the cause for your delay."

"Thank you for everything." Rhiannon rushed out the back door, past the sleepy scullions trying to wake up in time to make bread for the morning meal.

Ian was already in the stables waiting for her, having finished preparing for their departure. She noticed him first with George, and then the second saddled horse.

The disappointment at seeing the second horse was a bit of a shock for Rhiannon. She'd gotten used to cuddling up to him while they rode, but also, this was a blessing. Desire was heating up between them, and they were better off separately riding so they weren't touching each other all day. Maybe that would help to cool whatever feelings she had growing inside her.

She just needed to get north. Needed to see her cousin. Start a new life. And they didn't need any distractions along the way. Fighting off her brother, her betrothed, outlaws, and traitors was quite enough, thank you very much.

Rhiannon attached the satchel of borrowed undergarments to the saddle, ignoring Ian's offer to help her. He knew very well that she could get up into that saddle on her own.

Besides, from here on out, she needed to avoid touching him altogether.

Touching him only led to more thoughts of touching him, which led to heated stares and almost kisses. As it was, he'd seen her practically naked, and she hadn't even cared. She'd wanted him to look. If that didn't spell trouble, she didn't know what did.

Rhiannon snapped her fingers, and Goosie jumped up onto her lap. She stared at Ian, his jaw tense, and she ignored the urge to reach for him and attempt to calm him.

"Shall we, my laird?" she asked.

Ian smirked. "Indeed, my lady, we shall."

He flicked his horse's reins, and they headed out into the darkness. She might not have been able to run well, but riding was a different story.

8

The sun had yet to rise as they headed out of the inn's stable, eyes and ears keen for any sense of movement in the shadows of the village. Every tree became a potential swordsman, and every roaming dog a scout.

Ian had taken out half a dozen men at the tavern. Mostly, Scots who seemed down on their luck and had taken the bribe from Rhiannon's betrothed or brother. He'd offered every man an out, but they were blind to his proposition when they had a bounty they desperately wanted to cash in on.

Though none had given the name of the men who sent them to attack, it wasn't hard to guess it was Adam and his would-be brother-in-law because all of them, before their eyes rolled in the back of their heads, cursed the *Sassenachs* who'd promised them a big reward. And really, he couldn't blame them for seeking a higher fortune than he had to give. Poor bastards had risked their lives without realizing how much they were getting into trying to fight Ian. Though he'd warned them, what reason did they have to believe Ian when he said he was one of Scotland's greatest warriors?

And then there was Rhiannon.

Ian's gaze roved over to where she rode beside him. The lass rode astride, her back straight, hands on the reins. Goosie was tucked into an empty saddlebag, her head poking out for a second before ducking back into her hiding place. The saddlebag for the cat had been the wee stable hand's idea, and Ian was pretty impressed as he'd not thought of it himself. Goosie seemed content to curl up inside.

Just as she handled knives well, Rhiannon appeared to be an expert rider. At least at this slow pace as they sneaked free of the village. The truth would be revealed when they were out on the road. Rather than exiting through the main gate or the rear of the village, they left by way of the side, where most of the folk brought in their animals during storms. It was a small gate, rarely used, and not one, he guessed, the enemy would observe. He hoped the English would assume they would go out the front or the rear.

As they exited, he looked around, trying to make out every shadow and lump. When it was clear they were safe, he beckoned Rhiannon to follow. They would head out to the road by way of the fields, skirting around any ambush and then going on their way north.

The fields were wet from rain, and this required them to go slow. Their horses' hooves sank deep into the mud, making sucking sounds with each step as they pulled their hooves out of the muck.

They took it slow, and he remained cautious. At least they had the nighttime darkness as somewhat of a protection, but even in the moonlight, if he gazed across this field, he'd be able to glimpse any lurkers, and the English could also spot them.

Breath held, words silent on their lips, they slowly made their way across the expansive fields until the road was in sight. Still, he bid them pause, looking up and down the road, trying to remember exactly every bend in the road, every massive rock or tree, so he wouldn't mistake a band of men for what his brain recalled was an outcropping of fir trees.

At last, he felt they could move on, and he nudged his horse's flank and nodded to Rhiannon. The road was drier and more compact than the fields, and they were able to pick up the pace. Rhiannon kept pace beside him, her body moving elegantly with the horse in a way that made him wish it were lighter so he could observe the beauty of her movements. Blast it all, but getting two horses was supposed to help him with his desire. However, it only seemed to make him want her more. Now he could see her, watch her, and she was a feast for his eyes, sending a million inappropriate thoughts running rampant in his mind.

Ian shook his head, trying to force himself back to reality. They were on the run from the enemy. Rhiannon had thrown a knife through a man's foot. If they didn't get clear of said enemy, she was going to end up tossed over a *Sassenach's* lap and hauled back to England, where she'd be forever a prisoner of some brute.

There was no way he was going to let that happen. Aye, it was true. He couldn't have her for himself, wouldn't let himself have her—he'd sworn off commitment, and wanted adventure—but that didn't mean he didn't wish her all the happiness in the world. And a life that didn't involve being suffocated by rotten men.

Just because the road ahead of them was clear didn't mean they wouldn't run into any English as they went. And he needed to keep his wits about him, else they would find themselves in the center of an ambush he should have seen forthcoming.

The enemy had to be lying in wait somewhere as they waited to find out what had happened with the men they'd paid. They needed to hurry to avoid them altogether—or at least put enough distance between them before their attackers realized they'd skirted around them.

Ian picked up the pace, urging his horse into a gallop. They needed to get a few miles away before he'd feel comfortable slowing down.

Again, Rhiannon kept pace.

He sped up.

So did she.

Ian grinned into the darkness. Mayhap they should make this escape into a little bit of a game. At the very least, this would help the time pass. And at the most, he'd enjoy the hell out of a little challenge.

He sped up again. She followed suit.

"Are you wanting a race?" Beside him, she flashed a grin that promised she'd give him the contest of his life.

"How fast can ye go?" He wiggled his brows in an open dare.

"Any pace you set, Laird Ian Sinclair."

Lord, but the way she said his name sounded sweet as pie, and he nearly groaned from thinking about what his name would sound like on her lips as he kissed her and made love to her. *Nay. Nay, nay*. None of that. Focusing on the race and the thrill it would give would hopefully scratch the itch his desire thrust upon him.

"Ye asked for it."

"Did I?" she taunted.

Ian's grin widened. He supposed that if they were going to be in a race for their lives, they might as well enjoy it. He urged his horse into a full-out gallop, and Rhiannon kept pace beside him. They raced down the road, putting distance between them and their enemies at neck-breaking speed.

A quarter of an hour went by like that, with Rhiannon pulling ahead, her body braced over her horse's neck and Goosie poking her head out to find out what her mistress was playing at.

Ian didn't try to catch up. The view from behind was mesmerizing. He would have painted her like that if he knew how to paint. Her glorious hair flying behind her head, the sun just starting to rise, lighting the world anew, and the smile she tossed behind her—one of triumph, one of confidence. My god, he'd never seen a woman so beautiful before.

"Ye win," he said, and he didn't just mean about the race. She was winning him over second by second. A dangerous combination of desire and dreams.

"Oh, really, laird?" she teased as she slowed down so he could catch up. "And here I thought you were a man of adventure."

It was as if she were speaking to the silent part of his thoughts, the ones that warred within him about his exact desires to do just that—adventure—and the other part that was starting to long for Rhiannon to be his. And that part needed to be laid to rest.

As mesmerizing as she was, as much as he wanted to lift her off that horse and splay her out on the slowly warming grass beneath him, that would be a complete twist and turn of his lifelong intentions. A betrayal of his vows.

Ian was not his brother. He could not be his brother.

Noah was the one who'd settled down. Had a wife and a bairn on the way. That was his way of life. But not Ian's. And Ian didn't want it. He wanted adventure. To be able to leave whenever the wind blew. Ian planned to pass the Orkney Isles onto all the bairns that Noah and Douglass had together.

But what if he didn't? The tiny voice inside him slithered around, painting pictures of him and Rhiannon at his castle.

Pictures of them riding horseback along the shore. Frolicking in the waves. Feasting, dancing, playing. He imagined them making love in his bed. Rhiannon round with his bairn, with more children surrounding them.

It was absurd. And Ian decided to chalk it up to lack of sleep.

After all, when was the last time he'd had a good night's rest?

"The only adventure we're going to get is some distance between us and the enemy and a camp in the woods tonight where we can rest before continuing." His voice came out gruffer than he wanted, and he flicked his gaze to her to see if he'd hurt her feelings.

He was not a man to apologize for his actions typically. Yet, for some reason, when it came to Rhiannon, he was making all sorts of changes.

She was not offended, and instead was laughing. "Now you're just being a sore loser."

"I am no' a sore loser."

"The only adventure we're going to get is some distance between us and the enemy..." she mimicked him, her throaty voice deep and her face full of mirth.

Ian rolled his eyes. "I ought to take ye over my knee and give ye a good walloping."

"Would it make your loss feel less...loserish?" She pressed her lips together in an obvious attempt to stifle a laugh.

"Is that even a word?" he grumbled.

She shrugged. "It is now."

Ian chuckled. "Ye're something else."

"I think you mean, a winner."

"Aye, a winner." A beautiful, enticing winner.

"And what shall be my prize? Hmm..." She tapped her chin, her gaze moving toward the heavens, which were thankfully clear of clouds, as the sun lit their surroundings. A day without storms would get them some good distance.

"I didna know we were racing for prizes."

"What would a man want as a prize?" She cocked her head toward him.

Ian raised a brow. He knew exactly what he would have asked for. And her lips on his would have been the sweetest prize of all.

Rhiannon gasped. "I can see what you're thinking."

"I assure ye, ye canna."

She laughed. "Oh, but it was written quite plainly on your face."

Since when had he displayed his desires too plainly? Ian prized himself on having a face that gave away nothing of his feelings, and now this woman could read his thoughts. Impossible.

"What was I thinking then?"

"Oh, I couldn't say." She ducked her head, pretending to be scandalized, for he was certain this lass didn't have a shy bone in her body.

"I want to hear it."

"You would." She snickered.

"Aye, that's what I said."

"Well, then, if you insist."

"I do." God, he wanted to hear her say it. Every inch of his skin reached forward as if he could elicit the words from her throat.

"You were thinking that you'd ask for the best prize of all —the chance for Goosie to be in *your* saddlebag because you are so incredibly jealous that I get to have this momentous moment with my cat, and you've always wished that you had a cat for a companion." She ended with a laugh that could have made flowers bloom.

Ian's mouth fell open. The lass had quite an imagination,

and by the way she looked at him with humor glittering in her eyes, he knew she was teasing him too. Mercilessly.

But he decided to play along with her because why not?

"I canna believe ye found me out. I have indeed always wanted a cat for a companion, and watching ye ride with Goosie so comfortable in her new lodgings, the wee thing's head popping out of the top of the saddlebag, did indeed put me into a jealous fit of rage as I watched. I am filled with sorrow as I've no' had that experience yet in all my days."

Rhiannon's head fell back as she laughed, making his body hum with desire. And he'd been the one to make it happen. Saints, but she was stunning.

"How about this, my laird," she teased, "the moment you beat me at a race, we will transfer the kitty bag, no questions asked."

"We have an accord, my lady." Ian held out his arm to shake on it.

Rhiannon stared for a minute, then reached out, her palm sliding over his as she gripped his forearm with a strength he'd not expected. Her touch sent shivers up his arm, and he wished he could make them stop.

Her gaze met his, and he could only think that she must have felt it too.

They rode on in silence after that, each alert to the sounds of the road and taking it slow when more hiding places than clear pathways appeared. But as day turned to night again, they had yet to come across a single enemy. Not wanting to test their good fortune, Ian decided they should make camp.

He led her into the woods, deep enough away from the road they wouldn't be seen but not far enough away that he might not hear someone approaching. They set up a makeshift camp, burning a fire only long enough to cook the squirrels they caught. Then he stomped it out so they might get some sleep. They were lucky the scent and sight of the smoke hadn't yet drawn anyone to their position. But as Rhiannon rose from the fire, she wobbled and fell against him.

Without hesitation, Ian caught her in his arms, the weight and warmth of her exactly as he'd guessed it would feel. And he let her sink against him, her bottom fully on his lap, her arms rising around his shoulders to balance herself. Her breasts pressed to his chest. The weight of her against him, the softness of her body, made it hard to breathe.

"Oh, thank you," she whispered. "I'm so sorry. My foot must have fallen asleep while we sat here. When I stood up, it was all numb."

"Is it awake now?" he murmured, staring down the length of her skirts.

"I think so." Rhiannon lifted a leg, twirling her ankle about.

The hem of her skirt fell back slightly, revealing more of her boot and causing Ian to stiffen as the urge to take her boot off had him gritting his teeth. Again, those damning questions were in his mind. What would it be like if he allowed himself a little leeway? What would a life with a woman like Rhiannon—nay, not like, but the woman herself —be like? Was a kiss, was more, worth breaking his vow of bachelorhood?

"I can feel my toes again," she said softly, her eyes wide as she stared at him questioningly.

But neither of them moved. He didn't want to let her go, and she didn't seem in a hurry to stand.

"We should get some rest," Ian said, swallowing hard, a reminder to them both of where they were and the dangers they faced. And still, neither of them moved.

"Aye," she said softly, her fingers gripping his shoulders.

And then she issued a great sigh as if she, too, were fighting the same internal battle.

She moved to rise, but Ian held her back, not ready to let go.

"My laird?" she asked.

"Aye." Reluctantly, he stood, lifting her with him and setting her on her feet. Still, they didn't part, toe to toe, their bodies touching, her hands still on his shoulders.

"Ye know I wasna thinking about the cat," he said, referring back to the race and what the prize would have been.

"I know. Because I wasn't either."

Ian's gut tightened along with the rest of his body. He shouldn't have admitted that, and she shouldn't have answered. Yet here they were in the middle of a darkening wood, their heated bodies pressed together and hours of pent-up energy from racing away from the enemy to desire pouring through their veins.

There was only one way to release it, and that one resolution wouldn't do. If they let go, if they gave in, everything between them would change. And even if they somehow made it through a kiss to move on with their days, Ian knew he would be forever changed in a single moment.

"We canna," he said.

"I know." The disappointment on her face was exactly the way he felt.

"I'll take the first watch," he said.

She started to turn away, and when he thought he would finally be rid of his raging desire, she turned back, lifted up on her tiptoes, and kissed his cheek. Her lips were soft against his flesh, her breath warm, and his face burned where she touched him.

"Good night, and thank you," she said.

Ian cleared his throat, which had suddenly grown so thick he wasn't certain he would be able to find his voice. "Good night, and ye're welcome." It took everything in him, including fisting his hands at his sides, not to pull her back toward him and kiss her senseless until they both sank to the forest floor and finally released the tension between them in pleasurable wave after pleasurable wave.

9

A kiss on his cheek.

What a coward when a few inches more and she could have kissed him on the lips. It had been a reckless and last-minute decision, one which she'd retreated from and skirted his mouth for the plane of his face.

Rhiannon was restless that night as she tried to sleep in the tent Ian made for her. The ground wasn't especially comfortable, and the moment she thought she'd found a good spot, her hip or shoulder would start to twinge. She'd shift to the other side and feel the same thing there. Or when on her back, her lower spine argued with her about that position. And all through that, her mind ruminated, refusing to let go of the rampant thoughts of Ian. Of her future. Of everything and anything.

Who knew that the power of one tiny gesture would have the ability to shake her to the very core? That his cool cheek, slightly covered in stubble, would send shivers trembling over her skin and create a sea of unending turmoil?

Thoughts of Ian haunted her dreams, but they weren't all

good. Nay, it was arriving at her cousin's castle to find the land burned, the castle destroyed and endless bodies until she reached her beautiful cousin, her body crumpled and Rhiannon's missive in on her chest with a knife stabbed through it. Ian, trying to save her and being murdered by her brother's henchmen.

She woke drenched in sweat despite the chilly early morning air. Sticky clothes clung to her; if she weren't in the middle of a wood, she'd have shredded them off for relief.

Rubbing the cobwebs from her face did nothing to smooth away the horrors of her dreams. Images flashed relentlessly in her mind, replacing the early morning forest views that peeked from the tent flap opening.

Outside the makeshift tent Ian had put together for her, she could hear him moving around. And while she wished she could hide inside forever and not face the man she'd spent all night thinking about, her body screamed for her to get up and move, if only to work out the kinks of sleeping on the hard ground.

So, she climbed out, spotting him rolling up his blanket and attaching it to George's saddle, which he'd already put back in place. She stared at his back, trying to find the words to tell him they had to hurry, that her cousin was in danger. But he already knew the dangers and wouldn't put stock in her nightmares. Ian seemed more practical than superstitious.

As soon as he turned around and saw her, his brow furrowed, and he looked at her with great concern. "What is it, lass?"

"I...I didn't sleep well." She rubbed her hands through her hair, feeling the tangles at the back from tossing all night.

His lip twitched into the merest smile. "I dinna want to sound offensive, but I can tell."

"I'm sure I look a fright." She touched beneath her eyes,

which were puffy and tried to smooth her mane of hair. Short of dunking her head into the closest river, it was unlikely she'd be able to tame her locks into submission with a few strokes of her hand. And the swollen undersides of her eyes, well, only a good night's sleep was going to help with that.

"No' a fright. Never a fright. Ye look as if ye've been haunted, though." The wrinkle between his brows didn't disappear as he watched her, waiting as she tried to find words.

"I was. My dreams…I think they may be a sign of what's to come." She explained seeing her letter brutally stabbed to her cousin's chest with a dagger. "I sent three missives, and you said Douglass only ever received one. That means there are two more out there, and I wouldn't put it past my brother to have intercepted them. That means he knows where we are headed. He's been unable to cut us off on our journey there, so he may plan on reaching there and killing everyone before we arrive."

Ian walked toward her, reaching out, his heavy hand a comfort on her shoulder as if the weight of his touch would ground her somehow. At the same time, she was so tired, so overcome with emotion, that the feel of him, the reassurance in his gaze, punctured a hole in the dam holding back her tears. She wanted to collapse against him, to feel the comforting weight of being held by someone.

"Lass, I assure ye, no matter the size of your brother's army, he'll no' get past Sinclair walls. My brother's, now your cousin's, castle is heavily fortified. Second, my brother's men were trained by me, and though I havena met your brother or the man with whom he intended to settle his debts by way of ye, I can guarantee they are no match for the warriors I helped to train. There will be no slaughter. When we arrive, ye'll be able to wrap your cousin in your arms."

His words were spoken with such confidence. Not a waver, not a wobble, and he looked deep into her eyes. He believed all of the things he was saying, and oddly enough, she believed them too. Even still, that dam of tears was ready to flood, slipping down her cheeks in silent surrender.

She was so exhausted. This journey had been a lot harder than she thought it would be. And she'd tried to be strong. She *was* strong. But sometimes, even the strong had a moment of weakness when their emotions undid them.

Ian clucked his tongue and pulled her against him. She collapsed into his warm and solid embrace, her cheek to his chest where his heartbeat thudded in a steady rhythm. He stroked her back with an expert hand, his chin on her head as he murmured assurance. From the gentle way he handled her, and the way he so easily sought to soothe her, she knew he was a good brother. A good man.

"Thank you," she murmured against the wet spot she'd left on his shirt. "I'm sorry for falling apart."

"Never be sorry for letting your emotions out. We all need to do it now and then." There was a weight behind his words that made her want to pry.

Rhiannon peeked up at him. "Have you cried?"

Ian chuckled. "I'm a man, men dinna cry." His tone had an extra helping of bravado.

She pretended to give him a little punch, and he chuckled.

"I admit to having cried at least once, but I'll never admit to the true number of times." A cloud fell over his face then, the jovialness gone. But he quickly shook it off and grinned again, though it hardly reached his eyes as if his smile were trying to break free of the darkness.

Whatever haunted him, he wasn't willing to let it come to the surface. And she respected his desire to keep it hidden, even if she was curious. "Once is enough," she said and leaned her head back to look up at him more fully, a smile finally finding its way to her mouth. "I hope you never have cause to cry again."

Ian smiled down at her, and in that moment, time seemed to stand still. The heat of every other moment boiled down to this one embrace. His touch had been meant to comfort, and it was now shifting into what they'd been trying to avoid for days—desire.

She'd been irritated with herself last night for not kissing him. What was the use of letting him go this time?

Rhiannon clutched onto his shirt and lifted on tiptoe. Ian didn't push her away; in fact, he seemed to be moving with the same urgent speed as her. Both needed to forget the overwhelming emotions that threatened to undo them.

Their mouths crushed together in a heated frenzy, all the pent-up desire and need and wanting bursting out of them in this one kiss. Lips on lips. His hands pressed her back, holding her close, and her fingers curled into his shirt. Their breaths were heavy, fanning over their cheeks. A swipe of his tongue, and then she deepened the kiss, wanting more and more. To come apart in his arms and forget her nightmares. Forget the dangers of the past few days. The betrayals of her brother.

All she wanted was Ian and this moment to last forever.

Holding Rhiannon in his arms seemed the most natural thing in the world. The softness of her body pressed to his, the warmth of her touch, the smell of her hair. When she'd come out looking as if she'd lived through a night of war, he'd been concerned. When she'd told him of her nightmares, her fear for her cousin who was more like a sister to her, Ian had felt that in his bones.

He and his brothers had been through hell together—

especially when Ian had been taken, held hostage years ago in a dungeon of a neighboring clan. He knew exactly what an emotional war felt like, and he wanted to take all of her fear and pain and toss it deep into the flames of a bonfire, where it would disintegrate to ash. Holding her, hugging her, comforting her had not even been a thought. It had been a reaction.

And as he held her, he couldn't help but think that this right here was everything right in the world. When she'd looked up at him with the same heated stare he'd been trying to avoid for days, he knew he was toast.

She'd leaned up, and he hadn't even hesitated in slanting down. In brushing his lips over hers. Within half a second, it became clear she knew how to kiss and wanted this kiss as much as he did. The both of them were fully intoxicated by the desire they'd held at bay, which had now been unleashed into a torrent of roving lips and clutching fingers.

Ian held her close, pressed one palm to her lower back and the other to the back of her hand where she clutched his chest, his fingers threading through. He wanted to hold her there forever. To taste the sweetness of her mouth for the rest of time.

Holding her, kissing her, letting himself go in this moment of frenzied passion was the last thing he'd *thought* he wanted. The last thing he'd thought he *needed*. For the better part of a decade, he'd believed that surrendering to a heat like this, to his desire for a woman, would only hold him back. Yet as he crushed her to him, claiming her mouth in one heated swipe of his tongue after another, Ian couldn't help but flash-back through every moment they'd had together that led up to this point.

And he didn't find one moment she'd held him back. If anything, she was his equal. A dagger-throwing hellion who didn't run at the first sign of danger but was prepared, willing, and able to save his arse.

With Rhiannon, he'd experienced adventure. She dove headfirst into it as he did. Was it possible that...maybe a woman like her wouldn't hold him back?

She whimpered against his mouth, and the blood running through his veins sizzled right down to his groin, where his cock hardened.

His brother was happy with Douglass. More than happy. Besotted. And it hadn't seemed to lessen the toughness of him. If anything Noah fought fiercer now.

Because Noah had more to fight for than himself and principle. He had love.

Ian groaned, with desire and maybe a little fear. Because though he wasn't ready to admit, deep down, a part of him was starting to fall for Rhiannon. To imagine a life where the two of them could be together. A life of adventure and passion.

He should push her away. Deny the thoughts and feelings tunneling through him. But it was as if fate or the gods had taken over his body because instead of telling her no more, he kissed her harder.

It was only the slight sting at his ankle that made him pause in his devouring of her mouth.

"Ouch," she said, and that got his attention.

The two of them pulled back, eyes glassy, lids heavily lidded. Then they both stared down to see Goosie between them, scratching first his ankle and then hers as if using them both for a scratching session.

"Stop that, silly Goosie," Rhiannon cooed, bending down to give her cat a pat on the head.

"Saved by the cat," Ian murmured with a chuckle.

"Saved?" She raised a brow at him. "And what were we in danger from?"

"I'd rather no' say. But kissing often leads to it."

Rhiannon's cheeks heated, but she didn't look away. "I am not naïve, Ian, though I am..." She pressed her lips together, not finishing the sentence. He knew what she meant.

The lass might know how to kiss, but she'd yet to make love.

Ian crouched down, giving Goosie a little stroke on her back, the cat wrapping her tail around his hand.

"I would never call ye naïve, lass. And ye're a verra good kisser."

"Thank you." She lifted her chin, a small smile of satisfaction on her lips. "I'd say I've had a lot of practice, but that's probably not ladylike, and it also makes it seem as if I may have...done other things, which I have not."

Ian chuckled. "I understand. I do hope that whomever ye practiced with was a gentleman."

"He was, if he could be called a man."

"And is he in your life still? Perhaps the reason ye did not want to marry your brother's suggested groom?"

"Nay. Just a lad from my past. My brother's suggested groom was a cad and a brute. I'd be nothing more than a broodmare to him. I would never have wanted to marry him. I didn't know him, and my brother kept me hidden when he came to the castle, yet I knew what kind of man he was by how he treated the servants." A shudder passed through her that he wished he could take away.

"I've met men like that before."

"But alas, the lad I kissed before is long gone from my life. Years ago when I was barely a woman. I fell in love." She shrugged.

A little stab of jealousy probed at his chest as he imagined a brightly fresh-faced Rhiannon falling in love. But to be honest, he was glad to have the grown woman here with him. Spirited and brave, a combination that made her both lethal and amusing. Ian had never met a woman like her. She could play and tease and, if necessary, do serious harm in an ambush.

"Is he still alive?" Ian asked, referring to the lad who'd been able to kiss her first.

Rhiannon tossed him a saucy smirk. "Why, are you jealous?"

Ian chuckled. "Wondering if we'll have yet another army following us to Scotland."

"Ah, no. My uncle saw to that. Put a stop to our relationship as quickly as he could. But he is still living."

"Devastating."

"I was gutted at the time, but now I see the wisdom in it. I wasn't old enough to be in that situation. Practically still a baby."

Ian grinned, his eyes roving to her very womanly lips again. He'd like to kiss her again. To pull her down to the ground and see what other things she might enjoy. But alas, Goosie had done them a favor because if they didn't hit the road now, there was no telling how fast the enemy would be upon them. They still had days until they reached Castle Buanaiche, but fortunately, they could stop at his brother Alistair's castle, Dunbais, on the way.

"Well, woman," he teased, "we need to break down camp and hit the road."

Rhiannon chuckled, flashing him a mirthful look. "Aye, *sir*."

Ian couldn't help the laugh that burst from him at that. "I deserved that."

Rhiannon scooped up Goosie and deposited her into the satchel attached to her mount, and Ian shook his head, still amazed that they had a feisty cat on the trip with them. If a fortnight ago Noah had told him that he'd soon be traveling with a cat and a woman who could throw a dagger better than most men, he'd have laughed him out of the castle.

Life worked in mysterious ways. For there was another revelation Ian had discovered: perhaps he wasn't as satisfied in his solitary life as he'd previously believed.

❧ 10 ❧

Despite their heated morning, the rest of the day, they barely spoke. Riding hard on the road, then slow through the woods when Ian spotted a caravan or other riders ahead. No matter if they were in Scotland now, he wanted to avoid anyone on the road who might put them at risk.

They'd had to sit quietly hidden for half an hour at one point as a long trail of merchants passed on the road. Goosie had jumped from the satchel, winding her way through the crowd, and Rhiannon had winced the entire time. But either no one noticed the cat among them, or they assumed she was a stray.

Rhiannon was grateful that Ian was so intent on keeping them hidden as they traveled, even if it were from a group of merchants who would hardly cause them harm. And with his careful tactics, they weren't detained along the way and made a good leg of the journey into Scotland. The deeper they journeyed north, the more the weight that had settled on Rhiannon's shoulders started to lift. Each passing hour was an hour closer to her cousin. To safety and an escape from the fate her brother had laid out for her.

However, just like the night before, tonight they were going to have to camp in the open rather than find a place to rest their heads at a tavern, given what had happened last time. And while Gavin and Sarah seemed used to strife with their inn being on the border, Ian didn't want to bring any more danger to innocent people, which she completely understood and respected him for. Despite all his wild bravado, Ian was, deep down, a very caring man.

They made camp—a single makeshift tent for her, as he explained he slept better outside without being covered. Though her movements were slow, showing her exhaustion, Ian seemed to have endless energy. She helped to remove the horses' saddles, settling them on the ground for seats and stroked her horse's body, neck to flank. The sweet animal sighed with pleasure at the break. Goosie, the only one to have rested well on the ride, took off for a hunt.

Rather than risk a fire tonight, Ian pulled some of the provisions given to them by Gavin and Sarah from his satchel. Bannocks and jerky. Rhiannon settled on her saddle, a blanket on her lap for warmth, and chewed thoughtfully on her jerky as she glanced at Ian. The man was handsome. Wild hair, stormy eyes. Everything about him exuded power and allure. And, oh my, he kissed like a dream. She'd never been kissed like that before—with such fervor, such passion. There was a big difference in kissing Ian, a man and warrior, and the adolescent son of a neighboring lord. Her belly did a little dance as she thought about how her breasts had pressed to his thick chest, her mouth melting on his. She wanted to kiss him some more. To toss her dinner and slide onto his lap.

She hoped that she'd arrive at her cousin's castle soon— and she didn't want to think about how many more days were ahead of her, even though she needed to know. Because if she had to stare at Ian's face for much longer fantasizing about kissing him more, she was liable to stand up, yank him up, and give herself over completely.

But that one time would have to be enough. Decadent memories. She hadn't escaped one unwanted marriage to fall into another one, no matter how handsome he was or how delicious his kiss was. She wasn't ready to commit herself to someone. Not yet.

Rhiannon just needed to get to her cousin. To be safe. She could think about her future later.

"How long is our journey?" Talking about anything but kissing was necessary to pull her mind from her wanton pondering. "I've never been to Scotland or the Highlands before."

"'Haps another day or two to my brother Alistair's castle. We'll rest and get cleaned up there, restocked on provisions, and then a few more days to Noah and Douglass's."

Blast... There was still so much time. Perhaps that was the wrong question to ask.

"Oh, that will be nice." And it would. Staying with Alistair meant fewer nights on the road and less time alone. Plus, there was the added benefit of possibly bathing at the castle. Days of travel dust covered her skin, and her gown could use a good scouring. She was grateful for Sarah's extra chemise and hose, so at least the clothes right next to her skin felt cleaner than her gown. But still, all of her and those items could use a good soak and scrub.

"Aye, and 'twill be a night we dinna have to worry about anyone sneaking up on us."

She nodded, glad he was honest about the dangers since she'd been thinking the same thing on the road with him. Her eyes roved around the slowly darkening forest, imagining outlaws lurking. Behind the castle walls, she'd always felt safe. And even when she roamed, she'd always had a guard, like now with Ian. Not once had she ever considered how precarious safety could be and how easily it could be swept away until her brother had eviscerated the last remnants of her naiveté.

"And a hearty meal," Ian said. "Alistair's cook is one of the best. Probably could make this jerky taste like a fresh roast."

"Oh, is that so?" Rhiannon's mouth watered a little at the idea of a fresh roast. Besides Sarah's delicious stew, she'd not had a warm and savory meal in weeks since her brother had not seen fit to advise his cook to make one for her. Just crusts of bread and cold porridge.

"I've tried to lure him back to Orkney, but he wouldn't go, and I suppose that's just as well since I'm never there anyway and Alistair would likely kill me for it." He tossed a piece of jerky into the air and then caught it in his mouth.

"Impressive," she teased, and he answered with a grin and a wink. "Why are you never at your castle?" She bit into a dried Bannock, crunching.

Ian looked away, seeming to study the trees, but she thought he was avoiding eye contact. "I was for a little while, but..." He let out a short laugh. "It may sound dumb to ye."

"Try me." She chomped on another bite.

"I was bored." He shrugged. "I know that is no' really a good answer, but 'tis the truth."

Rhiannon gasped a laugh. "Bored? Bored being the man of the castle?"

"No' much was happening." He popped the cork on his water-skin, took a long swallow, and then passed to her. "We're a ship's ride away from civilization. The Vikings are no longer attacking. 'Tis a rather peaceful existence."

Rhiannon savored the cool water on her throat, which

was dryer than she'd realized. "And you're not a peaceful man."

"Hardly," he snorted.

Returning the cork to the water-skin, she passed it back. "I noticed that. I can see where a man with your spirit would grow restless."

"Restless, aye. I rebuilt all the crofts, bigger and stronger. I redesigned my castle, even stacking stones and spreading mortar myself on the extended outer walls. But none of that was what my body longed for. I hosted games, organizing great feats of strength and prowess. But winning at games is different than battle. I needed more."

She cocked her head, watching him as he spoke, dissecting the movements of his body with the words from his mouth. From her observations, there was a great deal of guilt with his decision to leave, and at the same time, a great deal of satisfaction. "And so, you left?"

"I did. I have a wonderful second in command who I left in charge, and I went to Noah and asked if I could train his men. Mine were already trained and would continue to hone their skills with the games while I was gone. The isles are run well, and I thought, if I didna keep up with my training in the world, what good would I be to them?" Ian ran his hand over his face as if wiping away his guilty thoughts. "It sounds selfish when I say it aloud, but I truly believed that I was helping my people by leaving. Staying abreast of what was happening in Scotland, rather than being isolated in our relatively safe world."

"If you believe it was making you a better leader, then there's nothing wrong with that. I don't think it sounds like you left simply because you were bored."

He leaned back on his elbows, totally relaxed. "Perhaps not. Thank ye."

"And your brother, he probably appreciated the help."

"I believe he did."

They finished their dry dinner, and Ian passed her a flask this time rather than the water-skin.

Rhiannon shook her head, pushing it back. "I don't like spirits."

"It will help ye sleep tonight." He took a long pull.

Well, that was enough to convince her. She was utterly wiped out, and she could use the rest after the night of sleep she'd had previously. If this was going to help, then down the hatch. She took the flask, practically choking down a big gulp. The spirits burned on the way down, heating her belly, and almost instantly, she felt...lighter. And so, she took one more gulp and put herself to bed.

In the end, it wasn't the nightmares that woke Rhiannon, but the shivering. Without the fire and the summer coming soon to a close, the nighttime air grew colder, seeping into her bones until the thick wool blanket felt like thin muslin. Her teeth started to chatter, and she rubbed her hands together, then wrapped herself tighter into her wool blanket, but she couldn't get warm. The cold had taken root in her body, laying siege and refusing to vacate.

The flap of her tent moved, and she jolted up, afraid she was about to be attacked, but it was only Ian poking his head in. "Your chattering teeth are likely to alert any roving wild-cats." Though the words were teasing, his tone was concerned.

She grinned around her rattling teeth. "Goosie didn't seem to appreciate it either." Her cat had left at some point, perhaps part of the reason Rhiannon was no longer warm and snuggled. The animal was particular about her sleep, and Rhiannon couldn't blame her.

"Let me help warm ye up." His words were perfunctory, all serious. And though part of her knew she should protest, the freezing half agreed wholeheartedly, her body already leaning toward him, seeking warmth.

Ian sank behind her and pulled her into his arms. An instant wash of warmth on her back made her push harder against him. He tucked her legs between his, an arm around her waist, her head under his chin. A cocoon of safety and heat. She snuggled deeper and sighed as parts of her body began to thaw.

"My goodness," she said, her teeth starting to chatter less. "You're like a campfire yourself."

He chuckled, the rumble going through her back to her chest. "It is one of my good qualities when it's cold, not so much when it's hot."

Good quality or not, she was already feeling better. The chattering and shivering had subsided, and the feeling started returning to her fingers and toes, which she wiggled. She sighed into the glorious feeling of defrosting and thanked the heavens for things like campfires, castle walls and maybe hot-blooded warriors. If she couldn't have the former two, at least she had the latter.

"Thank you for this," she said through a massive yawn. "I feel so much better already."

"I'm happy to help, lass. Now, get some rest. We've another long day, and I dinna need ye falling off a horse."

Rhiannon yawned again, sleep already tugging her into its grasp. "I'd never fall off a horse."

"Until ye do."

She smiled, her eyes closing as the warmth she was surrounded by made her eyes heavy. She could get used to this. Lying in Ian's arms to fall asleep. The cold fought back by the warmth of his large body. Feeling safely tucked in. Sensing they were together, or perhaps glad the chattering had stopped, Goosie slipped back beneath the tent's walls and curled up next to Rhiannon, her purring drawing Rhiannon into a deep sleep.

WITH RHIANNON'S LUSH BODY SNUGGLED UP AGAINST HIM, Ian lay stiff as a board—in more ways than one. At first, the chill of her had seeped into his skin, the shivering and chattering numbing him. But the coldness quickly melted into a warm bottom and plush breasts that rested against the top of his arms.

He didn't want to shift and feel the round of her hip, the subtle indentation of her waist. Already, it was a torment for her long legs to be between his own. At first, he could ignore the pleasantness of having her so close, but then, as her body filled with the heat he shared, there was no more ignoring.

The soft swell of her arse was pressed tightly to his groin, and if she wiggled one more time, he was liable to lose his mind.

Her soft snore was the only thing that kept him from kissing her because she needed sleep, and so did he. Except just before the dawn of the most pleasant sleep he'd had in ages, he was woken from a dream where Rhiannon had her leg wrapped around his hip and her breasts pressed to his, her breath on his neck.

Only it wasn't a dream.

Ian's eyes widened to find the woman splayed over him, their bodies touching in such an intimate way that were they unclothed, they'd be a mere inch from him taking her innocence. She was still asleep, and he didn't want to move in case he woke her, but he could not stand this torment.

He slid to the left with a subtle shift, but even that small movement had her stirring, a little hum in the back of her throat. Her eyes fluttered open, blue and heavily lidded, as if she sensed him watching her. She smiled lazily, as one does when first awoken from a pleasant dream. He refused to think of another reason she might look up at him like that. One that involved no clothes and a night of undulating limbs.

"Good morn," she murmured.

Ian cleared his throat and then grunted. Afraid to speak or move. The desire he'd had for her the night before was still there, tenfold. And he was a mere inch from her, seeing how hard he was for her.

"Thank you for helping me last night. I've not slept so well in a very long time." She stretched, arching her back and pressing herself more against him, and then she gasped, her eyes flying toward his as her hips surged forward and felt the evidence of his desire he'd been trying to hide.

She might have been innocent in that she'd not yet lain with a man, but that look told him she knew exactly what an erection was.

"You..." She started but then bit her lip.

Neither of them moved. Their eyes locked. A mountain of thoughts passed, cultivating into one thought he couldn't stop repeating: Just one more kiss.

He knew that kissing her was a mistake—especially in his current state—but this would be the last one. In a couple of days, they'd be at Alistair's, and he could put real distance between them. Get back on the right path. Back to his future as a bachelor. To protecting Scotland and training others without the sweet torment of her as a distraction.

Until then—they had this moment for him to have one last taste.

Ian leaned in and captured her mouth, damning himself as he did so. As soon as their lips touched, a bolt of lightning struck, and he lost all sense of what was right and what was wrong.

Rhiannon eagerly kissed him back, their tongues finding

each other in the middle as they slid easily back into the frenzied, passionate kiss they'd shared before. God, how he loved the taste of her. Couldn't get enough of her. If things were different, he wouldn't hesitate to make love to her over and over.

If things were different.

But they weren't.

Yet, he still kept kissing her. Rolling her onto her back and pressing himself against her. Rhiannon moaned as she gripped her leg, wrapping it more tightly around him, allowing him to press the hardness of his arousal to her heated center. Ian groaned, shockwaves of pleasure rocking through him. Why he did that, he had no idea, other than instinct, because now all he could think about was sliding inside her. Claiming her.

The very last thing he should be doing.

Rhiannon was not meant for him, even if lying here like this, kissing her as though his life depended on it, felt so right. It was so very wrong.

Her hands slid over his shoulders, kneading the taut tension he harbored there. The weight of worlds seemed to melt away with her touch.

"This is madness," he murmured against her lips, kissing her gently over and over. "I canna want ye like this."

"I cannot either," she said, her fingers sifting through his hair as she kissed him back.

"We need to stop," he groaned, kissing her harder.

"We do," she panted.

But they didn't. If anything, telling each other they needed to stop only made them kiss more. And then his hand was slipping beneath her gown, his palm skimming the softness of her calf, the dip behind her knee, and she whimpered with pleasure. Ian groaned, his fingers pressing into the back of her thigh.

All right, that's it. He forced himself to cease kissing her, shoving himself back onto his knees, his arse hitting his heels, and then he practically threw himself out of the tent to get her out of his line of sight. All sense of control had abandoned him, and that seemed the only way to gain some of it back.

Rhiannon's surprised gasp echoed in the early morning, along with an angry cat mewl. He found himself staring into the eyes of Goosie as if the feline were judging him for what he'd done or maybe how he'd ended it. Wide yellow eyes, slitted black in the center. The black hair rose on her back. She hissed at him as if to say she was disappointed in his behavior.

Ian muttered an expletive under his breath and shoved himself to standing, marching a dozen paces away with his cock rock hard. He unlaced his breeches, took himself in hand, and finished the bloody business, praying it helped relieve him from the curse of desire.

But even as he spilled his seed, even as pleasure wracked his body, it felt empty. What he wanted was to be fully sheathed in the woman he'd left breathless in the tent. He cursed again, louder this time.

What was she doing to him? Not in his presence for more than a sennight and she'd already irrevocably changed him, made him question his entire philosophy on life, his future plans. How?

Ian returned to camp to find her munching on a Bannock, her cheeks still rosy from their intimate embrace, but otherwise looking as peaceful as anyone might on a beautiful summer morning in Scotland.

"Feeling better?" she asked, a slight smirk to her lips. Did she know what he'd just done?

"Nay," he growled, snatching the Bannock she held out.

"Too bad." She popped the last of her breakfast into her mouth and then started to take down her tent.

He didn't understand her. Couldn't be sure if she mocked him because she knew more than she was willing to say or if it was in her nature to tease. It didn't matter. He felt a like fool either way, because in just a matter of days, the lass had been able to take down his defenses and leave him completely vulnerable.

Ian had not lain with a woman in years. On purpose.

"Ye," he started his accusation to tell her she'd put a spell on him.

But she turned to face him, a brow raised, a smile on her lips, and the words stilled on his tongue. Rhiannon was the most intriguing and gorgeous creature.

"Thank ye for doing that." He pointed to her tent. "Let me finish."

"I can do it." She didn't stop either, still moving around.

Ian shook his head, standing and taking over the work. "I know ye can, lass. Ye've proven yourself more than capable in so many things. But ye shouldna have to. Let me. I want to help."

"Why not? Because I'm a woman?" Hands flew to her hips, drawing his eyes, and he forced himself to swallow the groan.

"Aye."

"Women can take down tents."

"Aye."

"So why is that the reason?"

"Because ye shouldna have to dismantle the place I nearly ravaged ye in." His voice was a little louder than he intended.

"Ravaged, eh?" The laugh was evident in the lilt of her words. "Is that what you call it? I rather like that word."

Ian swallowed, tamping down the need to ravage her once more. This woman was going to drive him mad...

"We need to get on the road," was his only reply, for he feared what he wanted to say—that if she wanted a ravaging, he'd give her a good one that left her legs shaking and her heart pounding.

Rhiannon's laugh tinkled through the forest like a fairy's as she saddled her horse, then mounted the way he wished she'd mount him. She tapped her lap, and he wished he were Goosie jumping up to lay right there. When she caught him staring, the lass actually had the audacity to wink.

She knew what she was doing to him. There was no question of that.

Even if he knew it was stupid, Ian decided that the best way to keep himself from snatching her off her horse and having his way with her was to ignore her completely.

A feat that proved harder than he thought. He barely spoke to her, only offering grunts instead of words. She chattered on anyway. By noon, she hopped off her horse as if she'd not been riding for hours and pranced off to relieve herself. They sat for lunch, and still, she talked. And talked. And teased. He said nothing.

By the time they made camp, he'd decided an ocean between them was probably necessary, and at this rate, he would go all the way to the Orkney Isles. Was this a trick of some sort? Was she not in trouble? Had his brother connived him into picking her up and bringing her to Scotland with her, driving him to return to the one place he didn't want to go?

"What is your purpose in going to Scotland?" he asked, certain now she was up to something—though he knew full well that believing she'd begged for an escort to seduce him was utter rubbish.

She cocked her head. "Have you been tippling the flask?"

"What?"

"You know exactly why I'm going to Scotland. To escape

my vile brother and his despicable attempt at marrying me to that slimy lord." She narrowed her eyes. "Are you unwell?"

Ian groaned. "I'm perfectly fine."

"If you say so." She shrugged. "I'm going to sleep."

"I'm no' going to warm ye."

"Your choice." She rolled her eyes and disappeared into her tent with Ian feeling like an arse, which he was.

11

P eople were confusing. Men even more so, especially when they got ideas into their heads. Rhiannon could not be one hundred percent certain what had gotten into Ian's, but she did have a tiny inkling.

The man was mad.

Mad for her, she suspected. To be fair, she was mad for him too. Their kiss, the way he'd touched her, the slide of his body on hers, the way it had felt to have her hips wrapped around his, the hardness of his arousal as he pressed against her most intimate place. The sounds of his breathing, the low growl of approval when she'd kissed him back, still echoed in her ears. All of what had happened haunted her the entire day. That was why she'd been unable to stop talking about anything and everything if only to distract herself from... herself.

And, it appeared, she was better at hiding her feelings than he was. The man was positively a grouch.

Aye, she was way better.

Ian stomped around their camp; before that, he'd stomped every time they stopped. As if the act of stomping would squash his inner turmoil. He even made it seem as if his horse were stomping as they trotted along their course.

Poor man was positively riddled with guilt or regret, though she wasn't sure why because as much as he had ravaged—a word she rather liked—her, she had ravaged him as much. Or maybe that was the issue—he wished he'd not done it. Which would be surprising given his enthusiasm.

Not since her fling with the lad ages ago had she felt so... elated. As if she were floating, and her body sizzled. When she saw him, smelled him, she wanted to touch him. To be touched. Every inch of her tingled, reaching, wanting.

At first, she'd chalked it up to the excitement of adventure. The thrill of something new. Maybe even a little bit to falling for the man who saved her. After all, there had to be some feelings for the man who was taking her away from an unwanted future. And he was very handsome. His body was rock solid, which seemed unfair to any other man.

But his body, or even the striking cut of his jawbone, wasn't why she liked Ian. Why she wanted him to kiss her. It was the way he looked at her—eyes full of interest and admiration, a little teasing and even better when they flashed desire. The way he talked. The way he joked. The way he respected her. The way he nodded with approval when she threw her dagger. Ian made her feel like a real and whole person, which wasn't always the way it was for women. She knew that, just as every other woman did. Just the way women also knew that it was their lot. They were the birthers of babes, the caretakers of the men, the runners of the household. How dare she dream of anything more? And yet, Ian seemed to commend her for being different.

So, besides his incredible body and being the kind of kisser that made her toes curl, Ian made her feel good on the inside too. Until now, that wasn't something she knew she wanted.

And she suspected she made him feel the same way. Or at least she hoped.

Having spoken with him and knowing the reasons for his running from his responsibilities in Orkney, she supposed she understood why he would want to push her away now. A man on the move didn't want to be entangled. And she knew first-hand that kissing was a complication. The only question was, how long could she hold out before she demanded he quit this nonsense and kiss her again?

What if he held out forever?

What if she never kissed him again?

Or maybe the better question was: what did she want? A husband? Rhiannon frowned. That was not what she had wanted a few days ago.

She slid her glance toward Ian, watching him frown into the horizon. The problem was she didn't know what she wanted. Until he'd appeared at the edge of the forest, she'd desired to get away from her brother. To escape a fate that would have been pure misery. And even the first day on the road, she'd just needed to survive, putting one foot in front of the other. And now... Now, she longed for more. For a life that included a man who supported her interests, a man who cherished her. Could Ian be that man?

Ultimately, whatever happened between the two of them, whether it was to become more or less, she knew she wanted to be around him again. She didn't want their last kiss to have been in the forest under a tent with his calloused fingers massaging her bare leg.

Right here, right now, she wanted more than that.

By evening, her legs were starting to hurt, her rear long gone numb, and they still rode. She curled her toes in her boots, flexing her leg muscles and her bottom, trying to restore the feeling into them, but nothing helped. With days still left to ride, she wondered if she'd be able to walk by the end of this journey.

"How much longer until we make camp?" she asked, unsure if she'd get an answer since his predilection today had been to nod or shake his head or grunt—she suspected this was his protective mechanism against her and his desires for her.

"We're almost there."

"Almost where?"

"Castle Dunbais—my brother's holding."

"Ah, already." She'd forgotten about that and thought they had another day. Perhaps that was why her legs had gone numb—he'd pushed them past the breaking point. "That's wonderful." And she was genuinely happy because she'd been promised a bath, and she loved baths. She had high hopes that the warmth of the water would work some of the kinks out of her sore muscles. Besides, she felt so grimy that she practically itched to scrub herself clean.

No more than an hour later, the castle turrets came into view. Their approach slowly revealed the outer walls, the tall keep. There was the collective sound of men on the ramparts preparing for the impending intruders, and then Ian let out a shrill whistle that seemed to communicate the men could stand down. Rhiannon wasn't sure what she'd expected of a Scottish castle, perhaps one more rough-looking than those in England, but it looked about the same as Dacre. Stones were evenly stacked with mortar. The great doors were freshly constructed, judging by the color, and they opened wide behind an iron portcullis that had been raised. Ian nodded for her to go first through the entrance while he protected her back. It was the subtle things like that that she found endearing.

A moment later, they were being ushered into the bailey of Dunbais.

A warrior, the spitting image of Ian right down to the chiseled and stubbled jaw—which was rather shocking—trotted down the castle's stairs and jogged over to meet them. Ian's brother had a wide grin on his face as he wrestled his brother out of his saddle, the two of them joshing with each other until Ian remembered her presence.

With a slight clearing of his throat and a gesture toward her, Ian said, "This is Lady Rhiannon."

"Ah, we've heard much about ye. Lady Douglass was singing your praises when first we met." Alistair approached her side of the horse and held out his hand, a friendly smile in her direction. "May I help ye down, my lady?"

"Thank you." Not wanting to be rude to their host, she took Alistair's calloused hand and allowed him to help her down. "A pleasure to meet you."

From behind Alistair, Ian's face was blank; the only thing giving away a clue of how he might feel was the subtle twitch of his eye.

Rhiannon hid her smile, confirming in that subtle twitch that he did indeed harbor something of her feelings. Or, at the very least, he was jealous she'd taken Alistair's hand when she mostly fought against Ian's. Well, perhaps he needed to recognize his emotions toward her in his own good time. She was a patient woman. Sometimes.

Alistair took Rhiannon's arm and led her into the great hall, Ian following behind. Their host introduced her to the housekeeper, who led her toward the stairs. Rhiannon glanced back to where Ian stood talking with his brother, eyes on her. Heat infused her cheeks at the intensity of that stare, the way he followed her with his gaze. It was only at the nudging of the housekeeper that she turned away to concentrate on the stone circular stairs.

She was shown to a chamber, and a bath was procured. Her clothes were taken to be cleaned, and in the meantime, a spare gown was given to her to wear along with clean underthings.

The bath itself was luxurious. A ball of soap scented with lavender soothed her skin, and the scent calmed her. She stayed in the water until it turned tepid and then chilled, finally forcing her out. Gooseflesh covered her skin, which she rubbed away with a soft linen towel, grateful that some of the aches in her limbs had dissipated.

After dressing, she brushed her hair before a warm fire, feeling more alive than she had in days. It was amazing what a good scrub could do for the body, and what a hot bath could do for sore muscles.

A knock sounded at her door, and she called for the housekeeper to enter, but it wasn't the housekeeper.

Ian stood in the doorway, taking up all of the space. She swiveled to face him, brush in hand, which she almost dropped, catching it at the last second. All the breath left her as she watched him, that look on his face again, made her entire body tingle. He, too, had cleaned up, hair still damp at the ends where it hung loose around his face. Gone were his breeches, replaced by a full plaid, his knees naked at the hem, and stockings up over the thickest part of his calf. She imagined she could smell his spicy, clean scent across the room—in fact, that wasn't her imagination at all. She sucked in a deep breath.

"I thought I might escort ye to supper," he said.

"Oh?" She set the brush down and started to plait her hair.

Ian watched her nimble movements, his gaze concentrating so hard on her fingers so that he didn't look at any other part of her, including her eyes. He didn't set foot in her room, his boots firmly planted on the other side of the threshold.

"Aye. Alistair insists we feast together."

At the mention of a feast, her belly grumbled. There was a very good chance she'd out-eat every man at the table. "Hmm. I am rather ravenous."

Ian grunted. So, they were still doing that. Rhiannon bit the inside of her cheek to keep from laughing. If he wanted to grunt instead of speaking, she'd let him do it for a little longer.

She finished plaiting her hair, tying it off with a ribbon that matched the light blue gown she'd borrowed, then sauntered toward Ian, who stared at everything in the room but her.

When she reached him, touching his arm, he jerked back as if stung.

"Usually, an escort allows the lady to hold his arm, but I can see you don't want me to do that. Perhaps I should walk behind you?" There was a subtle hint of annoyance in her voice. She'd been patiently dealing with his prickly demeanor for longer than she might have ordinarily gifted someone with her patience. His showing up at her chamber had made her feel as though they were finally crossing that threshold.

"Aye."

"Aye, what?" She crossed her arms and tapped her foot. "Walk behind you?"

"Nay, ye may hold my arm." He stuck out his elbow and nodded toward it.

Rhiannon rolled her eyes. "Why, my laird, thank you ever so much for the kindness."

"My pleasure." He grinned.

Goodness, but she wanted to pinch him to make him wake up. Instead, she threaded her arm through his, trying to ignore the ripple of muscle beneath her touch, the heat of his body next to hers. She supposed if he were trying to ignore her completely, he wouldn't have come to her chamber to offer her an escort. She'd have to take the small win where she could.

The great hall was bustling with servants and Sinclair clan men, women and children. She was introduced to many who remembered her cousin Douglass and were happy to meet her. Surprisingly, no one seemed to mind that she was English, which had been something she'd worried about. Ian stood like a statue beside her the whole time, which was clearly not his normal way, as his brother Alistair and the other warriors kept giving him funny looks.

At last, she was seated opposite Ian, with Alistair at the head of the table between them.

The man would have to either keep his gaze on his trencher the entire meal or be forced to look at her. She rather liked that he might be tortured during the meal. And so, as she feasted on leek soup, roasted goose, Scotch pies, a thick slice of goat cheese, and freshly baked bread followed by a sweet Cranachan, she watched him closely.

Each time Ian met her eyes, he quickly looked away until she was certain her face was redder than flames, as each look sent a fresh wave of emotion—desire, irritation, yearning, all bundled up neatly into the heat of her cheeks.

Alistair filled her wine and his brother's, watching the two of them with interest. Funnily enough, though they were identical, she could tell the difference between the two of them with ease. Ian, for one, had a faint scar in the middle of one eyebrow and another along the right side of his jaw. Alistair had scars, but one was in the center of his forehead and another was on his chin. Ian's blue eyes were a little darker with a hint of sapphire around the rim, and he wore his dark hair longer. She wished she knew what Alistair was thinking.

But alas, it wasn't as if his brother would blurt out—

"Ian, what the bloody hell is wrong with ye?"

Or maybe he would.

"What?" Ian scoffed, lifting his wine glass for a heavy drink.

"I've no' seen ye so quiet, nor so broody, in all my damned life." Then Alistair glanced at Rhiannon. "Apologies for my language, my lady."

"No apology necessary," Rhiannon grinned.

"I'm no' broody," Ian growled, which only made Alistair laugh.

"Och, nay, no' at all." Alistair's sarcastic tone caused a few snickers up and down the table, and Rhiannon had to force another piece of bread into her mouth to keep from laughing.

Alistair leaned toward her and, with his hand cupped over the side of his mouth as if he were going to tell a secret, said loudly enough for Ian to hear, "Normally, my brother is the jovial one, cracking jokes."

"Is that so?" Rhiannon acted surprised. "I can't say I know that side of him."

Ian glared at her, and she laughed.

The jovial atmosphere continued, and after supper was done and a few games of dice played, exhaustion settled on Rhiannon so heavily she feared she'd not make it upstairs if she didn't go now. However, the idea of going alone left her longing to remain behind.

Alas, it wouldn't do to ask Ian to accompany her. Rhiannon excused herself to go to bed, and Ian stood abruptly, eyes on her, his face flashing several emotions she couldn't quite decipher before he washed them all away. Had he, too, been thinking it would be a shame for her to go to bed alone?

Everyone stilled, watching their interaction—especially Alistair. Rhiannon paused, for it seemed he had something to say. Too much to hope that Ian would ask her to stay up a little longer.

And then, as if Ian were choking on the words, he said, "Goodnight, my lady."

Rhiannon smiled softly at him, wishing she could tell him to relax. Wishing she could rub the tension from his shoulders. "Goodnight, my laird."

12

Ian woke the next morning with a headache.

Unlike many mornings when he woke at Alistair's with a headache, this was not from too much drink. He'd taken only a few sips of wine at dinner—albeit a few more like gulps—and realized that if he had any more, he was liable to end up in Rhiannon's bedroom, having thrown caution to the wind. At that point, he'd stopped imbibing completely.

And he was glad for it because as she'd stood to leave, every inch of him had commanded he go with her. Wherever the willpower had come from that bid him remain behind, he was glad for it, as he almost hadn't been able to summon it.

Nay, the headache he awoke with this morning was from frowning so damn much. Saints, but that was not the type of man he was. And his brother called him out for being broody because of the three triplets, Ian was usually the most jovial of them all.

Alas, being jovial, while typically second nature for him, was impeded when he was concentrating so hard on not being interested in the woman that he was extremely interested in.

Bloody hell... Rhiannon had well and thoroughly gotten under his skin. Both good and bad.

A splash of cold water on his face helped, as did the tisane he begged Cook for, who thought his condition was from too many spirits. Fine by him, as long as he got rid of the infernal pounding behind his eyes before Rhiannon joined him at the table for breakfast.

Their meal was a simple fare of berry porridge drizzled with honey and a dollop of butter, but one of Ian's favorites. There was even a trencher of bacon, which he took a healthy portion of. By the time he'd had his fourth slice, he was feeling marginally better, the pounding gone and replaced by a dull ache somewhere on the back of his skull.

And then Rhiannon appeared as he refilled his trencher. Dressed in another borrowed gown that showed the curves of her hips, the fabric bringing out the sky blue of her eyes, and her red-gold hair shined. Ian would have liked not to notice such things, but alas, it was impossible *not* to notice.

She was the most beautiful woman he'd ever seen.

When he thought of a painted portrait hanging over his hearth—she was what he'd like to see, the way she was now, entering a room, fresh-faced with a slight curl to her lips and a teasing sparkle in her eyes.

He stood, as did every other man at the table, watching as she approached. The dainty swish of her hips, her skirts flowing about her long legs. As she took her seat, Rhiannon stared at him. His throat was tight, too tight.

"Good morrow, my laird," she said, and he felt like a cad for not having addressed her first.

A beat later, he seemed to be able to work his throat again. "My lady, I trust ye slept well?"

"Aye. So much better than a tent." One of the servants placed her bowl of porridge in front of her, and the delighted smile on Rhiannon's face was contagious.

It also appeared to be the cure he'd been looking for with his headache, for the pain receded to near-nothingness.

"'Tis indeed. Bacon?" he asked, prepared to serve her as was polite.

"None for me, thank you. This porridge looks delightful." She popped one of the berries in her mouth.

Ian ate without tasting as she dipped her spoon and brought it to her lips, clearly enjoying the buttered and honeyed porridge.

"Ah, Ian, ye look better than last night," Alistair said, marching into the great hall. He clapped Ian on the back hard enough that Ian almost choked.

His brother brought with him the scent of the fresh outdoors, likely the rounds he'd done that morning before breaking his fast. Alistair was a hands-on laird, like their brother Noah.

It was the way they'd been raised, to take care of their own. To be involved. A leader couldn't always take the word of their seconds and other assistants as the way of it. One had to see with one's own eyes.

Even as he thought that, he grimaced, realizing that was what he'd been doing all these years. Aye, when he was at his holding, he was hands-on, involved in everything, but the rest of the time? He took their word for it.

The whole place could have burned down, and his people sailed for France, and he'd never know because he believed the letters that were sent to him. Letters he would have to read when he got to his brother Noah's castle—which was where they waited for him. From Noah's shores, if one looked out on a clear morning, the shores of Orkney could be seen.

And since, more often than not, Ian ended up at Noah's castle, that was where his people sent him updates. Probably hoping one day he'd hop on a ship and return more permanently.

Alistair settled at the table, grabbing a handful of bacon. After chewing a fair amount, he said, "The English were spotted on the road south of here. About two dozen of them."

"Bloody hell," Ian grumbled. Rhiannon had been right. Her brother must have intercepted the letters and knew her exact route. The man might be a gambling arse, but he could plan and read a map. "Headed north for certain?" He hoped that perhaps it was just another regiment of Longshanks's men.

"Aye. My scouts came to let me know they were headed north, and the crest on their shields was three scallop shells."

"That is our family crest," Rhiannon said softly. "It is Adam."

Ian bristled, clenching his fists. "Want me to take men out and head them off at the pass?"

Alistair chuckled. "Ye canna have all the fun. My men and I will leave shortly to see where they are headed. Likely no' here." Alistair glanced at Rhiannon. "Would your brother know about Dunbais by chance?"

Rhiannon shook her head. "I didn't know about it, so I doubt he'll have figured out there is a connection. My guess is that he's on his way to Buanaiche, which he does know about."

"See," Alistair said to Ian, "Ye can be on your way without fear that they are headed here."

Ian wanted to argue. A good fight was always a cure for what ailed him, and right now, thoughts of Rhiannon and his future ailed him plenty.

"I've already taken the liberty of having cook prepare ye provisions, and our stable master is preparing your horses. Do ye want to take some men with ye?"

Ian shook his head. "Nay. 'Tis easier to pass unnoticed

with the two of us. We'll be at Buanaiche in a few days. There's no way Adam and his army will beat us there. They dinna know the mountains as I do."

Alistair glanced at Rhiannon and wiggled his brows. "I was also informed that Goosie has taken charge of the stables and slain many a mouse who wished to steal the horses' oats. Any chance ye'll part with her?"

Rhiannon smiled like a proud mother. "Unfortunately, nay, my laird. But if I ever find myself this way again, I will endeavor to allow her to serve your horses once more."

Alistair grinned. "I hope we do see ye again, my lady. It has been a pleasure."

An unsettling feeling lodged in Ian's chest. Almost like... envy, not an emotion he was familiar with, but it was instantly recognizable.

Was Alistair flirting with Rhiannon? He glanced at them. There was an easy comfort between the two of them when conversing. Perhaps more than a slight pang of jealousy flowed through him. Ian frowned, feeling the pinch of pain in his head wiggle in warning, and forced his frown away.

"I would love that," she said sweetly. "You and your people have been so kind to me."

"We would not dream of anything else, my lady. Now, if ye'll excuse me," Alistair stood, grabbing another handful of bacon, "we've some English to fight off. Brother, I'll be seeing ye." Alistair grinned as they had when they were children, and he got to play a game while Ian had to remain behind to finish whatever bit of schooling he'd been resistant to.

Ian came around the table and embraced his brother. "Thank ye," he said genuinely. "For everything."

Alistair grabbed him in a headlock, rubbing his knuckles on Ian's head. "Always, brother."

Once they had finished their breakfast, Ian and Rhiannon

headed to the stables where their horses were waiting, saddled. George pawed the earth, ready for the wind in his mane, his master on his back.

They rode over the familiar lands, following a path Ian could travel with his eyes closed and his hands tied behind his back. Along the route, he chose places he was familiar with to relieve themselves, rest, and water the horses, including a stop at his usual clearing for a noonday meal of cold chicken. They were mostly quiet, each deep in their thoughts as the journey drew closer to the end. And when the sun fell to the horizon, he determined, after what had happened to them previously on the road, it would be in their best interest not to sojourn at the usual tavern he liked to hole up in. Better to stay out of sight so no one else could be bribed into giving them up, the cost being their lives.

Instead, he found a dilapidated croft he was also acquainted with. While it was missing half its roof, the other half provided decent shelter, and he could start a fire to keep them warm, at least through the night. Though the smoke would be visible, anyone coming across them and seeing the walls might think twice. Maybe.

Inside, the makeshift cot he'd left behind was still there, propped against the wall. The place looked as untouched as he'd left it on the way to England. "Ye can take the cot," he said, lowering it to the ground and shaking out the straw-filled mattress. "I'll take a watch and sleep on the floor."

Rhiannon wrinkled her nose. "Are you sure? I could take a watch while you sleep on the cot."

"Ye'll take a watch?" He tried unsuccessfully to keep himself from laughing.

"I admit to never having done it before," she said with a dainty shrug, "but how hard can it be?" At that, she approached one of the windows and peered out. "All clear."

Ian grinned. "There's a little more to it than that. How about we practice first?"

Rhiannon smiled back and lifted on her tiptoes in excitement. "Excellent idea."

They gathered wood and prepared a fire, their camp inside the croft cozier than their makeshift outdoor sites had been. After they ate the dinner that the cook had packaged up—bread and bacon (none for Rhiannon as she declined) and cheese—Ian led Rhiannon to the broken half door of the croft.

"Part of taking watch is watching. Hence the name. And the part ye got right a bit ago."

"Oh, how odd. I would never have guessed it was called a watch because you watched." She rolled her eyes.

Ian chuckled and nudged her with his shoulder. "Your sarcasm doesna go unnoticed."

She smirked.

"Watch for anything shifting or changing," he said. "That is, sight and sounds."

Rhiannon nodded, and he watched as she scanned the darkening areas around the croft. "So, it's really a watch and listen."

"Aye. When it's just moonlight or no moonlight at all, your eyes will adjust to the shadows. You'll be able to pick up on if something moves and changes or a new shadow emerges, but at first, all the shadows and murky blobs will look as though they are moving, closing in on ye."

Rhiannon nodded. "I can see that. The tree there has shifted to the left and the right now."

Ian snorted. "Aye. Get used to the sounds. Ye'll be able to identify the difference between the scurry of a wood rat and the crunch of boots. Or the silent and pausing steps of a deer versus the steadier steps of a horse. Or the rustling of Goosie in the gorse bushes."

"Is that why you put our horses in the croft? So, we wouldn't mistake the noise of an enemy for the noise of our horses?"

"Aye and nay. They are inside to keep them close, so they aren't stolen, but also so we know their sounds."

"There's quite a lot to learn about taking watch," she said.

"Aye. But with practice, ye'll be an expert."

"Do you think that Douglass's husband will allow me to take watch on the wall?" The way she said it, so serious of tone, belied the laughter in her gaze.

Ian laughed softly at that. "Ye can try, but I doubt it."

"Worth a shot." She winked, and his insides melted.

"I hear he does whatever Douglass asks, so ye may only need to have her put in a good word for ye."

She sighed. "It sounds as if he adores her."

"That he does. He is utterly besotted. And she with him. Seeing the two of them together has been quite a pleasure." And he meant it. Noah's happiness seemed to know no bounds, making Ian extremely happy for his brother.

Rhiannon nodded. "I'm looking forward to seeing it for myself." There was something almost sad in her tone that touched Ian.

He wanted to comfort her, to ask what she was thinking if she were willing to share, but he was also scared to hear what her answer might be because he had an idea that what she wanted was someone to love for herself, and while he wanted to be that man, he didn't know if he could be.

RHIANNON CONCENTRATED ON THE SHADOWS, A FEAT THAT was proving very hard when standing next to Ian. Every time she was around him, it was as if her body took over. All of her senses heightened. She slowed her breath, trying to quell the over-beating of her heart. She attempted to ignore his breathing or how his warmth sank into her skin.

But it didn't help. Being in his presence made her heart thump harder against her ribs, and her breaths came a little faster. Peering at him from the side of her eyes, she hoped he didn't notice her reactions. Even her hands were clammy, her fingers curling in, pressing her nails to her palms to ground herself. She rubbed them against her skirts and squinted into the darkness.

Focus.

"Well." Ian cleared his throat, something she'd noticed he seemed to do only around her. "If ye're going to take the second watch, ye should probably take first sleep."

Rhiannon drew a long breath, letting it out her nose, and then turned to face him. But that had been a mistake. Because he turned simultaneously, and their bodies were practically flush. Any ideas she might have had about maintaining propriety or distance or trying to ignore the way her insides quaked were instantly gone as if they never existed. "I'm not tired yet," she whispered.

Ian's eyes widened a fraction, the muscles in his jaw flexing. "Nay?" He sounded choked as if it were an effort to push out the single syllable.

She shook her head and took a step closer, the tips of her boots touching his. Soon, they were going to be a Douglass's castle, and she'd be pampered and hovered over by her cousin and likely not have a chance to be alone with Ian again. And she'd spent hours, days even, contemplating what she wanted out of life. The only conclusion she'd been able to reach was this: she was fairly certain she was falling for Ian Sinclair.

If he caught wind of her sentiments or even returned them a fraction, there was a good chance that when they reached the holding, he would leave her there and disappear, escaping as she felt him itching to do in the moments that she caught him staring.

The idea of him walking out of those castle doors and her never seeing him again made her chest ache. It was true they hadn't known each other long, but in the short time they'd been acquainted, they'd experienced more than some people ever did in a lifetime. There was a mutual understanding between them of each other's needs in life. A respect for one another's talents.

She'd never risked her life for anyone—but she'd done it more than once now for him. The truth was Rhiannon cared deeply for the man. Dare she even say this was *love*? He made her feel good, more than good.

She reached out, her fingers gently brushing his but not taking hold. A silent question. She'd never been this bold before. She peered at him through the fringe of her lashes, not to be coy, but because she wasn't certain she could face rejection if it were written on his face.

"Ian, I..." she started but stopped, biting her lip.

He drew a deep, shuddering breath but didn't push her away. His fingers threaded around hers. Calloused palms flatted to hers. Their intertwined fingers fit perfectly together. He touched her chin, tilting her face so she could no longer stare at him through her lashes but meet his gaze head-on.

"Make no mistake, lass," he murmured. "I want to kiss ye. I just dinna think I should."

Rhiannon wished she could wipe away his resistance. Of course, he was being a gentleman, and it was commendable. "You do not need to be a gentleman. We don't know what's going to happen. If we'll make it to the castle or not," she said. "And if we don't, I'll forever regret not taking advantage of this moment, of my...desire for you."

"And if I took the gift ye offered, ye may regret giving it to me in the morning." But even as he said it, he tugged her closer, where her hand was clasped with his, and he pressed it to his chest.

"I can assure you, I'd have no regrets. The only one I'd have is not taking this opportunity to have something I want. All my life, my uncle prepared me to defend myself and stand up for myself and what I wanted. And in one small moment of weakness, my brother took everything away. Imprisoned me. Decided my fate." She pressed her palm over his heart. "Before you came, I was already planning to leave. I'd sent my cousin those three letters, but I'd also packed a bag. The morning you found me, I was scouting the perimeter to see where my brother's men were, how far they would let me walk because, make no mistake, I was going to take my fate into my own hands."

Because he knew her so well, Ian didn't look surprised. He nodded as if he'd expected it. "I'm glad I was there. No telling what could have happened on the road to Scotland alone."

She smiled. "'Tis true. I was willing to risk my life and safety to escape, and you have certainly made the journey safer and faster. But please do not confuse my desire for you as some sort of...I don't know, some sort of payment."

"Och, lass, that is the furthest thing from my mind."

"Then...what is holding you back?" Rhiannon shocked herself at how bold she was being. How easily the questions came off her tongue. But it was only proof of how he made her feel. Alive and safe. She trusted him with her emotions and her body.

With Ian, she didn't mind being herself and sharing her thoughts. She didn't feel that he would censure her or judge her. He was invested in what she had to say.

"I thought I wanted to be an adventurer," he said.

Beneath her palm, she felt his heart beat a little faster.

"You are an adventurer, Ian. Look where we are." She glanced around the croft with its roof caved in on one side. "If this isn't an adventure, I don't know what is."

"For life."

The words were heavy with meaning, and Rhiannon tried to swallow her disappointment. She should back away now. Forget all of this and him. But she couldn't. Not yet. "I do not think kissing me takes away your sense of adventure." She smiled up at him, not a teasing or a shy one, but a smile that said she'd respect whatever decision he made. "If anything... you are tempting fate. Let's call it for what it is."

"I am." He slid his finger along her jaw, his gaze on her mouth. "Ever since I met ye, my ideas of what I wanted out of life, who I wanted to be...have been questioned."

"Not by me."

"Nay, by myself." He curled a tendril of her hair around his finger. "Change is no' always easy for me."

"For anyone."

"And yet, I find myself desiring change."

"Like what?" She stepped a little closer, her knees brushing his.

"Like maybe I dinna need to be wandering around Scotland searching, when what I want, what I have, is right in front of me, and right across the sea."

Rhiannon swallowed. She was right in front of him. His holding was across the sea. Did that mean he wanted her too? That he would take her back to his holding and...they would... Or was it simply that he had what he wanted in his holding, and that was what was right before him? Perhaps his words had nothing to do with her. And she hated that her mind was starting to question whether or not she'd made a mistake in broaching the topic.

"I canna claim ye, lass. No' until we've reached the castle and ye've had a chance to see your cousin."

He stopped abruptly, and she wondered if what he might have said was not until she came to her senses.

But all she heard over and over again in her mind was: *claim her, claim her, claim her.*

"You can kiss me without claiming me."

"I dinna know that I can." His gaze settled on her mouth, and she wondered if he was thinking about kissing her right then and there. She hoped he was. "And yet, I feel as if I already did. That by kissing ye, touching ye, I have already taken something that wasn't meant for me."

"You did not take anything, it was freely given." Rhiannon wanted to lean up on her tiptoes, to kiss him again and show him that it was her choice, that he wasn't some marauder of maidens or whatever such nonsense might be going through his head. "And I assure you, I am asking and willing to give."

Ian groaned, his forehead resting on hers, their breaths mingling, and still he held back. Rhiannon wanted to rush forward, to make this kiss happen, but the internal struggle he was wrestling with wasn't one she wanted to push him through. He was resisting her for his moral reasons, and if she were to shove those aside, to force him to do something he wasn't sure he should, then it would be her disrespecting his wishes.

And so, she stood there, holding him as he held her, his hand laid over hers at his chest where she could feel the erratic beat of his heart, and waited.

Gooseflesh prickled her skin. She bit the inside of her cheek. She tried to quell the pounding of her heart, but it seemed the more they stood there, the more they didn't move, the anticipation of what might or might not happen next grew tenfold, a thousandfold until she couldn't breathe properly.

When enough heartbeats had passed that she was certain he'd changed his mind and would step away and tell her they had to wait, Ian pressed his warm mouth desperately to hers. Claiming her in the press of his lips on hers.

The battle inside him must have been lost. But somehow, for her, it felt very much like winning.

13

This was a losing battle from the start.

A battle he was doomed to lose, and yet when he pressed his mouth to hers, he didn't feel as if he'd lost, but instead as if he'd been able to claim a victory. Ian felt he'd been fighting uphill from the moment he'd seen Rhiannon.

Rhiannon wrapped her arms around his shoulders, kissing him hard, and with equal fervor he paid her. Her body molded to his, and he held her close, stroking her back, her ribs, and then he risked cupping her breast. Waited for her to swat him away.

But she didn't. Instead, Rhiannon arched her back and moaned as if that were the one thing she'd been waiting for.

Ian was torn between what he thought was right and what he wanted. He desperately wanted her; he had never felt this way about a woman. It might be love, but his brother would never forgive him if he finished what his body desired, what Rhiannon had asked for.

More than that, what if he offered for her hand, and after a time in Orkney, the urge to disappear again reared its head?

A life with him was not guaranteed. How could he do that to her?

Ian stilled his kissing, his chest heaving with his breaths and his nostrils flared as he met her gaze.

"What is holding you back?" she asked, the words whispered against his mouth. "You can tell me. I'll offer no judgment."

Her words, the moment, disarmed him enough that he felt he could say exactly what he was feeling. "I want ye, lass, but more than just to slake my need."

She nodded, encouraging him to go on.

"I'm a wanderer." He shook his head. "No' in the sense of women, but in the sense of never feeling as though I can stay still. I have a need for adventure. I've never made my castle a home, and I dinna know if I could."

"Do you always adventure alone?"

The idea of the two of them riding off on the moors flashed before his mind's eye and brought a longing so potent he felt it deep in his bones. "Nay."

"Then what would stop you from bringing me with you?"

He had another vision of Rhiannon at the helm of his ship, her red-gold hair blowing in the wind. "Ye deserve better than that."

"But what if I, too, long for adventure?"

He'd not thought of that before. But it all made sense now that she'd brought it up. The lass was his equivalent in nearly every way.

"But I'll not force your hand or choose for you," she said. "I've made it clear what I want."

"I want it all," he murmured, eyes locked on hers, wanting every image of their future that danced across the landscape of his mind.

"I do too."

Mo chreach... He was well and truly lost now.

Ian's hands clasped her face, and his lips reclaimed hers. The way she slid her tongue over his, confident in her desire for him, drove him mad. Her lips were warm, luscious, and tasted faintly of the sweet tarts the cook had packed for them to eat after supper. Never had a woman so actively wanted him for him. Usually, it was for a place in his household, or to say she'd bedded the great Ian Sinclair. But Rhiannon genuinely wanted him. Knowing that and feeling her touch him, cling to him, made his head spin with want. Sensation and thought collided, tumbling through his mind and body.

The scent of Rhiannon surrounded him, intoxicating him. To think he could walk away now was absolute madness. There was no way he was going to give her up. To hell with adventuring alone. When the time came that she was ready to settle down, he would welcome it. If only he could kiss her like this every day.

With one hand on her hip and the other on the small of her back, he hauled her closer, tucking her body perfectly to his. The heat of her curves crushed to his body and had him letting out a feral growl, which she answered with a soft moan in the back of her throat.

Needing more and not caring what the consequences would be, Ian gripped her arse and lifted her in his arms, her hips pressed to his. A shock of pleasure made him shudder as his cock was pressed more firmly against her. He pressed her back to the wall, praying the damn thing held up. Rhiannon held on tight, her fingers clutching his shoulders as they both surrendered to the pleasure of kissing.

"Heaven, save me," he groaned as he sucked her lower lip.

"If saving means stopping, then I hope we are damned," she murmured, her breaths ragged and shallow.

Ian growled, low and feral, yearning pulsing through his body. His cock throbbed with the need to be buried deep inside her. How many times had he already denied himself the pleasure?

All he had to do was slide her skirts up to her hips, flip up his plaid, and do just that. He could take her right here against this dilapidated wall. The power of his thrusts were likely to make the entire place collapse.

But they needed to slow down. Taking her virginity against a wall not only seemed wrong, but he also knew, somewhere deep inside, that they could play this game as long as he didn't claim her wholly.

Ian slowly let her down but didn't stop kissing her. When her feet were on the floor, he held her arms above her head, keeping her captive to his kiss. Rhiannon moaned against his lips, pressing her hips against him, her back arching. Her desire enflamed his own. Ian slid his lips from her mouth, down along her chin to her ear, teasing the lobe as she squirmed against him. He pinned her hips to his, pressing her hard against the rickety wood.

His cock throbbed, hard as stone and pleading for the heat between her thighs. With the heat emanating from the center of her, he knew that sliding inside her would be sweet heaven indeed. Thinking to quell the blaze in his blood, he refused to put his mouth on hers. Her tongue was driving him wild. Instead, he continued his path of kisses over her collarbone, but then, he couldn't help himself; he moved lower to kiss above her plush breasts. She smelled of honey and tasted sweeter.

Touching her like this was enough to make him almost forget his vow never to spill inside a woman who wasn't his wife.

Letting go of her hands where he held them above her head, he slid the backs of his knuckles feather-light down her arms to her ribs. Stopping now seemed an impossibility as his control ebbed away. Slowly, he cupped her breasts, kneading them, brushing his thumbs over the turgid peaks as she gasped.

"Ian," she whimpered, her fingers clutching at the back of his neck.

The way she said his name, a mix of pleasure and surprise, sent a whirl of fresh desire through his body and straight to his groin. His cock strained, demanding he remove his plaid and claim the velvet flesh she offered. But he couldn't do that... At least not until they'd said their vows—if she'd still have him at the end of this trip.

Nay, but he could make her quiver, offer her exquisite pleasure. And though he hadn't lain with a woman for some time, he knew he was pretty damn good at making a woman's thighs shake.

Trailing his lips over the silkiness of her breasts, he breathed hotly on her flesh, licking in teasing little flicks. Rhiannon gasped, her fingers scratching at his shoulders, urging him on. With his teeth, he tugged the front of her gown down, revealing one rose-colored nipple and then the other.

His voice husky with need, he said, "Ye have the most beautiful breasts."

"Thank...you," she managed to say, her gaze on his, eyes full of lust.

Ian grinned up at her, keeping his eyes on her as he swirled his tongue over one nipple. "Och, lass, it is I...who must thank *ye*." Then he sucked her nipple into his mouth.

Rhiannon's passionate response was swift. She moaned, back arching, hips grounding against his, seeking, searching, and she tugged hard on the hair at the base of his neck. "Oh!"

Ian wasn't sure how much more he could take... He slid a hand down from her breasts to her hip, bunching her skirts up until his fingers skimmed the bare flesh of her thigh. She trembled against him as he stroked her higher.

Primal energy made his fingers itch to part her thighs. Daring fate, he caressed higher until his fingertips touched the heat of her quivering, damp core. Ian sucked in a breath as she gasped, both of them barely able to breathe. He stroked a finger between her folds, finding the nub of her pleasure. Rhiannon cried out, her hips jerking forward.

Ian kept his heated gaze on hers, his forehead pressed against hers.

"I can stop," he stated, knowing he could walk away right now. It would be painful, but he could. They could cease this insanity.

Rhiannon bit her lip, swallowing, pupils dilated.

"Don't stop."

As her lips formed the last syllable, popping on *p*, he thrust a finger inside her. Her channel was tight, squeezing against him.

"Oh, God," she gasped, at the same time he cursed.

She was so damn tight, her body holding onto his finger, and if it were possible, he would never, ever pull out.

Ian's control was going to snap and soon. He'd waited too long, he decided. That was the issue. He should have rutted every willing woman he encountered up to this moment if only to slake the need he was feeling now. He was going to burst, release his seed in his plaid from touching her.

He cursed again, dropped to his knees, and ducked under her skirts. There was only one way he could end this. To give her pleasure and then walk away before he took what didn't belong to him. Ian swirled his tongue swirled up her inner thigh.

"What are you doing?" Rhiannon gasped, her hands falling on his head from over her skirts.

"I want to taste ye..." he murmured.

He fanned his hot breath over the damp curls at the apex

of her thighs. Rhiannon lifted her skirts, her fingers gripping his hair tightly.

Then he reached his prize and kissed the very heat of her. She cried out, hips jerking forward.

He continued his sensual assault, his tongue swirling between the folds of her sex as he licked her into a sea of pleasure. Ian held her steady with one hand on her round buttocks, the other parting her tender lips while his mouth worked magic. He kissed, suckled, licked. Pushed her thighs wider apart, gaining better access to the slick, quivering folds and the nub firing pleasure and making her gasp his name over and over.

"Och, lass, ye taste so good."

She sounded as if she wanted to answer, to say something, but all that came out was a shuddering breath.

Her hips rocked forward, and against his mouth, her breaths grew quicker, her fingers in his hair tighter. And then, he felt it, the first vibrations of her release. Her sex quivered, spasmed, and she cried out, the sound enough to make even Ian shake. God, it was beautiful. As he licked her to the finish, he looked at her face, eyes closed, head fallen back, lips parted. She was stunning in her rapture.

Ian continued to kiss and nuzzle her sex until her spasms subsided. Her thighs trembled, as did her hands in his hair. At last, her breaths became even, and she gazed down at him, a soft smile on her lips, her cheeks red from pleasure.

"That was...delightful," she said.

He chuckled as he stood, dropping her skirts in place. His cock was still raging hard, and yet he felt a different kind of satisfaction.

"Might I give you the same pleasure?"

Ian's smile faltered, as he'd not expected such a question. "What?"

"Aye." She dropped to her knees.

And he was helpless to stop her as she lifted his plaid. His cock stood at attention, and she gazed at him so long he thought she might run away. He couldn't move, could barely speak as his body warred with his mind. Every inch of him wanted her to do this. To suck him until his knees buckled. But the logical part of his brain said a man would never let his woman do that.

Then she took his rigid shaft in hand, kissed the very tip, and Ian was lost. Doomed to whatever fate she had laid out for him.

Rhiannon lapped at him, her movements similar to how he'd licked her. He had to concentrate hard to stand. What would be worse, collapsing right here, or spending all over her? She tormented him with her tongue, growing bolder, swirling, and flicking around the crown. Then she licked him from base to tip before she nearly killed him by taking him into her mouth, sliding her lips down. Ian groaned, his entire body stiffening in ecstasy.

"I can stop," she teased.

Ian's eyes flew wide. He knew he should say, aye, stop, but he couldn't. "Och, nay, do no' stop."

She smiled and then took him deeper into her mouth. Bloody hell... This was utterly incredible and damned him to hell all at once. Up and down, slowly, she worked him into a frenzy. His hips rocked into her mouth with a rhythm steady and as old as time until he couldn't hold back anymore.

Ian yanked from her mouth as he cried out, taking himself in hand to spill his seed.

Rhiannon slowly stood in front of him, a saucy and satisfied grin on her face. "I believe you said you'd take the first watch?"

He laughed and nodded. "Aye, lass."

14

Rhiannon slept like the dead.

Who knew that pleasure was a sleeping aid?

When she woke the next morning, stretching on the cot as the sun shone through the missing roof, she rolled over to find Ian sleeping right beside her on the floor. A smile filled her face as she watched him sleep. The soft sound of his breathing, the fluttering of his eyelids as he dreamed. When was the last time he'd gotten a decent night of sleep?

He'd not woken her to take watch as he'd promised, and that was all right. Nothing appeared to have happened. And besides, with her luck, the moment he'd fallen asleep, and she stared out into the darkness, was likely the moment they would have been attacked.

Curled on her side, she studied him, thinking about how he made her feel so alive. Wanted. Even cared for. And how she reciprocated each of those sentiments in return. Desired for him to feel alive in her presence. Wanted him. Cared for him.

These were feelings that her cousin had told her about in

letters. Noah made Douglass want to burst with happiness. She claimed those feelings were love. Whenever she looked at him, she felt her breath leave her, and when he was out on rounds, she desperately wanted him to come back again.

Was that what Rhiannon was feeling now? Love? Or was it leftover euphoria from their pleasure-giving the night before?

Rhiannon pushed away the blanket, a smile on her face, certain that she was likely never to frown again. Memories gushed, flushing her skin with what she and Ian had shared the night before. She'd had no idea that what they'd done together could happen between a man and a woman. And it had been utterly glorious.

She stretched in the cool air, keeping as quiet as she could so as not to wake Ian as she slipped off the cot.

He'd been bent on pushing her away for days. Afraid to accept her desire. Until he wasn't. As she crept past him to go outside and find relief in the bushes, she wondered if today he'd change his mind. Have regrets. She certainly didn't, but she wasn't as troubled as he appeared to be from the start.

Beyond his decision to be a bachelor for life, one who sought thrills and rushed headlong into battle, there was a little something deeper going on. Almost as if he didn't think he was good enough to be someone's one and only. Rather rubbish, considering he was so incredible. But somewhere along the way, someone must have given him that impression.

As she squatted in the bush, a jingle of horses' reins had her clenching and freezing midstream. But her fears were immediately assuaged by the realization that Ian must have risen and was getting their horses ready to go. Of course, with his senses, he wouldn't have remained asleep as she snuck out of the croft. Finishing her business, she started to rise, her skirts falling around her ankles, but again, she froze.

The sound of horses wasn't coming from the croft but rather from the opposite direction, back toward the road.

Heaven help them.

They had company.

The blood drained from her face as the sounds of approaching riders grew. Every blasted curse word she knew went blazing through her mind. There wasn't enough time for her to dash back across the croft's yard and seek shelter.

Only a few minutes ago, she'd thought she'd be unable to drop her smile all day, but this wiped away her joy faster than a slap. In a moment of panic, she searched for Goosie, hoping her cat remained curled up on the cot where she'd left her.

Rhiannon remained crouched low, glad she'd slept in her clothes and boots. The dagger in her boot and the other still strapped to her wrist burned. If whoever was approaching didn't leave, she wouldn't hesitate to use one or both. Drawing in her breath slowly and releasing it, she worked to calm her nerves. To concentrate. She'd be no good to anyone if she made a racket or breathed so loudly that she could be heard.

Homing in her senses, she watched and waited, trying to discern exactly where the sound was coming from and how many riders were sneaking through the forest. Was it an army? A band of outlaws? Or simply a caravan of merchants as they'd seen before?

Dawn had barely risen, leaving the forest in hazy light. Anyone who traveled at this hour didn't want to be seen. And she should know, for they'd done the same thing.

With that knowledge in mind, she slipped the dagger from her boot. Faint movement in the trees beyond shifted the colors of the forest, and then it wasn't just the jangle of horses' reins but voices too. Spoken low in an effort not to carry, which failed, as she picked up the subtle tones of male voices. Several of them, at least.

They weren't English; she could tell that much. They spoke a mixture of Gaelic and English. *Scots*. Not her brother's army.

From what she understood, even the Scots weren't always welcoming to their own countrymen if they were caught on their land. Which meant that they were still in serious danger.

And she had no idea how far they were from Buanaiche, but Ian had said it would be several days, which meant it was very unlikely that these men were Sinclair warriors. But it was possible they were allies.

Rhiannon's brain was firing in a hundred different directions. Scenarios and plans for what to do in each blazing through her mind.

She wished she'd studied the maps in her uncle's office closer. Then she'd better understand where she was, but unfortunately, she was clueless. And all she could do now was pray the men moved along. Nothing to see here.

But they didn't.

The men came fully into view now. Maybe a dozen paces away from where she hid in the bushes. If one of them even turned to look in her direction and examined the bush a little closer, they would see her. There was only so much a thin bush could hide.

She counted three riders dressed in plaids on horseback. Unfortunately, she'd also not studied clan tartans and had no idea what the colors signified. What she could discern was that the coloring of their plaids was not the same as Ian's. A different clan. But she suspended judgment yet on whether they were friend or foe.

She glanced back nervously toward the croft for any sign of Ian or that they'd been there at all. From where she was, she could catch a glimpse of the horses through the broken wall, but not Ian. *Damn*. If they caught sight of the horses—

nay, when they saw them—they would know that trespassers were in there, and they would approach.

But to her surprise, they turned and kept on going. Didn't even bother with a closer inspection of the croft. Perhaps they were passing through on rounds? She waited several moments and then started to rise, to hurry back to the croft. When she reached her full height, a hand clamped on her shoulder, stilling her.

Rhiannon opened her mouth to scream, swiveling her neck to stab the ever-loving hell out of her attacker. Only to see it was Ian. He held a finger pressed to his lips for her to be quiet. Relief flooded to know it was him, and the scream died in her throat. When had he snuck up on her? She'd not heard anything.

Ian pointed toward the trees where the men had disappeared, but she was blind to whatever he indicated. Neither could she hear anything other than the rustle of the wind in the trees. But he was trained to pick up on things no ordinary person would. And she was happy to trust him since he'd gotten them this far and made it through his wild life with only a few scars to show for it.

A shrill whistle rent the air, and an arrow came whizzing from the forest beyond, stabbing at the ground right outside the croft, the shaft wobbling with force. Then a voice shouted, "Come out. We know ye're in there."

Ian made no sound. He didn't move. Rhiannon didn't either. They'd looked as if they were leaving, as though they hadn't noticed the croft was occupied, and yet, they had seen. Did they know she was in the bushes, and they were trying to mess with her sanity? A game?

But then, Goosie came trotting out of the croft, her interest piqued by the sound of the voice, the arrow. She sniffed it where it stabbed into the earth.

Rhiannon gasped, her body stiffening in fear. If not for Ian, she'd have bolted from the trees to save her beloved pet.

"A cat," someone called incredulously.

The men laughed. "The cat rode the horses in, aye?"

"Come out now, or we kill the cat."

That was the last straw. Without thinking or asking, Rhiannon called out, "I will come out. Please do not shoot. I mean no harm. And I want no trouble."

"What are ye doing, woman?" Ian growled. "Ye stay right there."

"Is that a *Sassenach* woman?" asked one of the intruders.

"Aye." Rhiannon jerked away from Ian's hold and came out of the brush, hiding her dagger up her sleeve so the men wouldn't see she was armed. Maybe if they thought it was just her, they would move on.

"Well, now, what have we got here." The sinister tone made her realize that no, seeing it was just her was not going to have them moving on. It was practically an invitation to stay.

"I am just passing through. Going to my cousin's," she said. "My cat and I will leave now and won't disturb you further. Good day, sirs."

They ignored her attempts to dismiss them. "Your cousin is Scottish?" The question was spoken with a great measure of skepticism.

"Aye," she lied.

"And ye have no escort?" They sounded very intrigued indeed, and not for any honorable reasons.

"I believe you met my escort. The cat."

Several men chuckled, and then whoever had been up in the trees and shot the arrow jumped down in front of her, his large, booted feet landing with a thud that rumbled the ground around her. He was massive, and for a second, she wondered how he'd gotten up in the tree at his size. The

Scot leered at her. "Did your cat ride her own horse, then, lass?"

Rhiannon nodded, not trusting her voice to keep Ian a secret.

"Well, that's not something ye see every day, eh, lads?" He chuckled, looking behind him.

Another man came out from behind a tree. He wasn't as jovial as the rest. There was a hard, mean look about him, and his gaze settled on hers was all business—or rather, all danger. "Cut the lies, lass. Where is he?"

"The cat?" She cocked her head and pointed toward Goosie, glad to see her hands only trembled slightly in her fear.

"No' the cat. Ye know who I mean. Ye didna travel all the way up here alone. No woman in her right mind would."

"Why not?" She hoped that stalling would at least give Ian a chance to figure out what to do. Though he was probably cursing her about now and wishing she'd given up Goosie.

"MacGregor." Ian's voice carried, and then he was there, brushing off his hands as if he'd finished working on something.

"Sinclair." The man's hard demeanor did not change. His eyes narrowed to threatening slits. "What the hell are ye doing on my land?"

"Just a wee stop on the way to Buanaiche. Dinna fash, man, we'll head out now, and ye willna even know we were here." Ian's casual inflection belied the tautness of his muscles. Instinctively, she could tell he was ready for a fight.

"What for? And with an English woman?" MacGregor gestured at her with a flick of his hand in her direction.

"My wife." Ian grinned. "I've just collected her from the land of the bloody *Sassenachs*." He passed her an endearing glance. "Apologies, wife," and then his gaze returned to MacGregor. "Headed to my brother's for him to meet her."

"I hate family reunions," MacGregor grumbled, his face pinching into disgust.

"They can be awkward," Ian said with a shrug. He was acting so casually and calmly that it was truly impressive because she could feel the intensity rippling off him despite his demeanor.

MacGregor grunted as he studied Ian.

Ian clapped his hands, breaking the awkward silence. "If ye wouldna mind, we'll get packed up and be on our way. We want no trouble. I'd no' want the lass's first experience with my fellow countrymen to be negative."

"First experience?" MacGregor glanced at her, his expression saying he wasn't buying a thing that Ian said.

"Well, first run in on the road," Ian explained before she could answer. "She's met Gavin."

MacGregor nodded. Apparently, Gavin, the innkeeper at the border was well known in Scotland. Fascinating.

MacGregor crossed his arms over his chest and stared hard at Ian for several assessing moments. "Ye'll have to pay the tax. No one crosses our land without paying the tax."

Tax? Rhiannon frowned. The man sounded like the troll under a bridge from the stories her uncle used to tell them when they were little.

"How about I fight ye for it?" Ian asked.

"What?" she said, unable to help herself from shouting.

MacGregor was grinning in a terrifying way, scarier than even his frown. It was a hungry, leering look. "Och, that'll do." He crushed a fist into his other palm, the smacking sound making Rhiannon feel nauseous.

"Nay, you cannot fight," Rhiannon said.

But Ian and MacGregor were ignoring her, the two of them having shed their weapons, and rolled up their sleeves, were now circling one another as if they were about to start brawling.

"This is madness."

MacGregor swung first, and Ian ducked. Then Ian swung, and MacGregor ducked. That went on for several ridiculous moments until MacGregor dodged and lunged, his shoulder landing in Ian's gut, and Ian grunted as all the air was forced out.

The men tussled to the ground, but this appeared to be exactly what Ian wanted, for he quickly gained the upper hand, rolling onto his back and wrapping his legs around MacGregor's thighs and his arm around the large man's neck. Pinned by Ian and scrabbling to grab the offending arm, MacGregor's face turned from red to purple.

"Say 'no tax,'" Ian said, "And I'll let go."

But MacGregor said nothing, still fighting the iron hold, until his face went from red to purple, and he lost consciousness.

Ian let him go, stood, and brushed debris from his clothes. The other men looked from one to the other, trying to decipher if they should fight in their leader's stead or let Ian go.

"I won," Ian reminded them, his arms out to the side, no weapons, showing he meant to fight no further. "We had an accord. Would ye fight me and go back on your laird's word?"

They looked at one another, then at MacGregor, then back to one another, then to Ian, and shook their heads.

"Good." Ian nodded, meeting each of them in the eye. "Stand back as we gather our things."

Ian took Rhiannon's hand and brought her into the croft. She followed his lead, her gaze behind her still disbelieving what had happened. And not at all trusting that the men would let them leave. Their horses were already saddled, as he must have done when she went to relieve herself in the bushes.

"Mount up," he told her, his voice brooking no argument.

And not that she would argue anyway. She wanted to get the hell out of here. Rhiannon swung up onto her horse and patted her lap, but Goosie jumped onto Ian's saddle. Fine, she'd put her into the saddlebag later. Ian did not mount his horse. Instead, he led them cautiously from the croft, their gazes on the men standing exactly where they'd left them. The fact that he'd yet to mount made her nervous. As if he fully expected another brawl and wanted to be able to move swiftly on his feet.

"The cat really does ride the horse," one of the men said, and they broke out into cackles.

Rhiannon patted her lap, and Goosie jumped over.

"Back away, lads," Ian said. "I trust ye to honor your laird's word."

They nodded, as their laird still lay unconscious, and they'd rather not deal with his wrath when he woke to find they hadn't done as they'd been instructed.

When they reached the edge of the small clearing, Ian mounted his horse, and Rhiannon put Goosie into her saddle-bag. Even as they rode out, Ian kept his eyes on the men, watching, expecting them to change their minds; no doubt, she certainly did.

But they remained where they were. A few minutes down the road, Ian glanced over at her. "We're going hard for a bit."

Rhiannon nodded and followed his lead, urging her horse into a faster pace. A short time later, they slowed, then went fast again. But after a few hours, the horses needed a rest from the grueling pace, and they stopped at a loch to give them water and a good rub down.

Their journey was like that for the rest of the day until nightfall. Rhiannon collapsed on the blanket she was wrapped in under the makeshift tent and was asleep the moment her head touched the ground. Ian woke her before dawn. They mounted up and rode out. The day was as the one before, and the night much the same.

But the following morning, after they'd been on the road for only a couple of hours, Ian pointed in the distance.

"Castle Buanaiche."

Through delirious eyes, she made out the shape of a fortress in the distance. Emotion welled in Rhiannon's chest, and she swallowed around the lump forming in her throat. She didn't think she'd ever been so happy to see a place. Tears burned her eyes, and she clenched her teeth to avoid bursting into a crying fit, which she felt very much like she might do. She was happy and exhausted, and because of that, a complete emotional mess. And, saints, but what a relief to finally be so close to her cousin. To have made it without dying.

"I can't believe we're nearly there," she finally managed to say, her throat still tight and the words strained with emotion.

"Just a wee bit more."

Rhiannon let out a long sigh of relief. The road to this point had been arduous and filled with fear. All of which she'd tried to keep tamped down so as not to go mad along the way. But now, everything was rushing out. "I want a bath. And a proper meal. Clean clothes. A game of cards or chess."

Ian chuckled. "I'm certain they'll give ye all that and more."

"And Douglass, I haven't seen her in so long." She swiped at the happy tears that dripped from the corners of her eyes.

"She will be verra pleased to see ye, lass."

"Thank you so much, Ian." She flashed him a smile, then laughed a little as she wiped away more tears. "I'm sorry to be crying. I am so grateful. I never would have made this trip on my own."

He grinned at her and winked. "Dinna apologize for your

tears. And it seems I may no' have either, considering how ye've helped me along with several foes now."

Rhiannon laughed. "'Tis true I helped, but I'm guessing you wouldn't have been in those situations were it not for me."

"Perhaps there is some truth in that, but I rather liked thinking ye a brave warrior woman."

"I'll not dissuade you from such thoughts." She glanced back at the castle, its towers rising through the trees, and beyond that, a massive body of water.

Ian's home was across those waters. They'd not discussed what had happened the night they were in the croft nor the confessions they'd made. Perhaps because they were both worried that the other might change their mind. She had not. A future with Ian seemed as much a dream as the castle standing almost within reach.

But the castle was there, and so was he.

She smiled at him and, without thinking, reached out to take his hand. Ian squeezed her hand in his. "Race you?"

He chuckled. "If ye dare."

Leaning forward in their saddles, they took off, laughing as they went. The Scottish air rushed through her hair. My goodness, the land was beautiful. Rolling hills and vast land-scapes. Mountains in the distance.

As they rounded a bend in the road, and she turned to Ian to declare her victory, but the look on his face made her go still. She followed the path of his eyes to see that a retinue of armored men was in the road ahead of them as if waiting for their approach.

From what Rhiannon had gleaned on this journey, the Scots didn't wear armor like that.

My god, it had to be impossible. But there they were clear as day.

English men.

They'd been beaten.

"Turn around," Ian ordered, and she did exactly that, following him at a breakneck pace, their horses already exhausted from the previous burst of speed but sensing their urgency, moving their hooves with haste.

"I know another way," Ian said, and she nodded, not wanting to risk speaking and losing her concentration or her grip on the reins.

The other way, he knew, was treacherous, down the side of a mountain. They dismounted and led their horses carefully down, the sounds of thundering hooves behind them.

Then they hid for what felt like forever under a rocky overhang as the English above them shouted orders and searched. Rhiannon pressed herself into the earth, becoming one with the dampness of the moss and leaves. She clutched her dagger so tight that the handle was bound to leave an impression on her palm.

"I should have known," Ian growled, cursing under his breath.

"We both should have." Everything before now seemed too good to be true, too easy. And now the English blocked their path to the destination she'd dreamed of.

More cursing. "My brother's scouts will have seen the English by now."

"They will fight?"

"Aye." Ian ran his hands through his hair. "I should be fighting with them."

The sounds from above moved on, and they waited until Ian was certain the coast was clear. They continued in the gulley they were in, hiding whenever they heard a noise until they came to a wide riverbed.

"We need to cross here, then up another crag, and we'll be there."

Rhiannon nodded.

"I'm sorry ye're going to get wet."

"I'm in for the adventure, remember? And I don't want to be caught by my brother and his men."

Ian grinned.

She tucked her skirts up and through the belt at her waist, ignoring Ian's wiggled brows at the sight of her legs. Then she removed her boots and hose and put them in her satchel.

"My god, woman, ye tempt the devil."

"Is that what you're calling yourself?" she teased and began walking into the water. She'd made it nearly halfway across with the water going up just over her knees, and then there was a distinct drop-off.

Thank goodness she knew how to swim. But sitting on her horse's back, Goosie was not pleased with her current situation.

"Stay put, kitty," Rhiannon said as her gown soaked up the water. She held tight to the stirrup, swimming and allowing her horse to drag her. The weight of her gown was cumbersome, and she wished she'd taken it off. That was something she'd remember for next time, she supposed.

They made it to the other side, and she climbed out, her gown felt as if it held half the water in the river. She wrung it out as best she could and then pulled on her dry hose and boots, grateful that those two things were not completely soaked.

They picked their way up another crag approaching the castle from the side. There wasn't much sound coming from the castle. She would have thought she'd hear the sounds of battle preparations, but Ian didn't seem concerned.

He let out a shrill whistle as they approached, crossing over a short field to a small drawbridge that was not lowered.

A man peered over the side and whistled back, then the drawbridge was lowered, and a door opened on the other side. Rhiannon's skin prickled. Again, this felt too easy, but moments later, they entered the side bailey, and the doors were shut and barred, the drawbridge raised.

"Rhiannon!" The shrill cry came from Douglass, and Rhiannon whirled around in time for her very pregnant cousin to crash into her.

They clung to one another, sinking in, neither able to speak for several moments.

"Thank God, you made it." Douglass's voice cracked with emotion.

Rhiannon clung to her. The tears she'd been holding back burst finally with relief and joy. "I can't believe I'm here."

"I can't believe you're here either. I prayed all this time that Ian would find you. That you'd make it safely back." Her words were spoken in a frenzied rush.

"We have made it, but I'm afraid not safely." Rhiannon swiped at her tears. "They are here. They followed us."

"Adam?"

"And the man he tried to marry me off to."

Douglass nodded. "When Noah's scouts spotted them, he knew you'd be here soon. They've been preparing."

A man who looked like Ian and Alistair approached, pulling his brother into a hug. Noah. The eldest of the triplets. Following behind him were two stunning ladies—she guessed them to be Matilda and Iliana, the younger sisters.

"Glad ye finally made it," Noah said, clapping Ian hard on the back.

"Are ye glad I brought ye some *Sassenachs* to play with?" Ian asked.

Noah grinned the same look that Rhiannon had seen on Ian right before he fought the large man in the forest. They were mad. Utterly and, without doubt, insane.

"Noah, this is my cousin." Douglass tugged on her husband's arm, and Noah faced Rhiannon with a welcoming smile.

"My lady, a pleasure to finally make your acquaintance. I've heard so much about ye, and I assure ye that your presence here has made my wife's dreams come true." Noah pulled her into a giant hug, and she smiled.

"And my sisters, Iliana and Matilda." The two ladies also pulled Rhiannon into a hug, which she greedily accepted.

"I hear ye're good with a dagger," the youngest, Iliana, said.

Rhiannon glanced at Douglass. "We both are."

"But how are ye with a sword?" Iliana raised a brow.

Rhiannon glanced at Ian. "I've yet to master the skill, but your brother has mentioned he'd teach me."

Ian laughed. "May no' be necessary, as any enemy of yours willna reach ye before your dagger pierces their heart."

"Or their boot," she teased.

"I need to hear this story," Matilda declared.

"I will regale ye with Rhiannon's heroics later when we've had a chance to clean up." He picked at a fleck of mud on Rhiannon's forehead to prove his point.

"Fair point," Matilda agreed and hugged her brother. "So glad to have ye back, Ian."

What a joy it was to have a family again.

Douglass gazed up at her husband with such love it made Rhiannon's heart ache with happiness for them both, and also because she wanted to look openly at Ian the same way.

"Good job, brother." Noah squeezed Ian's, and Rhiannon watched the exchange with a smile. There was much respect between the two. And rather than be sad for the brother she had who didn't show her as much affection, she was happy for them that they did.

"Do ye need a minute to rest?" Noah asked.

"I'll rest when I'm dead," Ian declared.

Rhiannon rolled her eyes as Noah nodded in appreciation.

15

Ian watched Rhiannon as she disappeared into the castle with her cousin and his sisters, who'd promised her a floral-scented bath, clean clothes and whatever she desired to eat.

"What's that look?" Noah asked, elbowing him in the ribs.

"Whenever I look at her, I have this odd sensation." He pressed his hand to his chest. "As if I might be having some affliction. I canna decide if she's good or bad for me."

Noah started laughing so hard he actually slapped his thigh. "Ye've got it bad."

"What?"

"Love."

Love? Och, nay. That was madness. Ian shook his head. Love was not a sentiment he knew how to possess—and if it were, he was definitely *not* in love. Was he?

"I never thought I'd see the day. Bloody hell." Noah faced the castle stairs, the door now closed. "Here we are on the brink of war, and ye're no' fighting for the hell of it like usual, but for something else."

"What?" Ian looked toward the doors, too, hoping the closed entry would somehow give him the answer.

"For Rhiannon." Noah jabbed him in the ribs again with his elbow and let out a snort. "I was fully prepared to lead Sinclair men into battle for my wife and her cousin, but I think ye're the one who needs to lead this. For the woman ye love."

Ian swallowed around the ache burning in his chest. Was this what love felt like? As if he might keel over? "What if she doesna want me?"

Noah shrugged and made a disappointed noise with his mouth. "Ye willna know unless ye ask."

"Ask her what?" For bloody hell's sake, was Noah suggesting he walk into the castle and tell her what he felt?

"Ask her if she'll marry ye." Noah rolled his eyes as if Ian had suddenly lost half his brain. "My God, ye might have come back from this trek a bit dafter than I thought ye were."

"Ye think me daft?" Ian jested, giving his brother a challenging look.

Noah tried to speak without laughing but failed. "As much as any other brother would."

Ian chuckled, then grabbed his head. "Saints, but I canna think straight when I'm around her. I dinna know if talking to her before the battle is a good idea."

"I think 'tis the right idea," Noah said. "Or else ye'll be thinking about it when ye should be focusing on slicing and dicing."

"Fair point," Ian conceded.

"Ask her if she'll wed ye when ye get back. Give her something to look forward to, and ye. She'll no' be as worried about ye if she knows ye plan to return." He shrugged. "Maybe. Och, maybe no'." Noah seemed to be worrying about his situation and working his way through that.

"Or maybe before we go, we should say our vows. Just in case."

Noah's eyes bulged. "Ye'd marry her right now? And wait a second, ye think ye might no' come back?" Noah pressed a hand to Ian's forehead. "I sense no fever. What the fok?"

Ian chuckled. "I am no' with fever, and there's no bloody way I'm no' going to win this. I think whatever is happening in here," he pressed his hand to his chest, "made me say it."

Noah stared at him, still in half-horror. "Get yourself together."

"I will. Promise. And aye, I would marry her now." Ian straightened his spine, realizing that he would indeed do that.

"I'll get Father August."

Ian nodded and marched toward the castle with purpose. There was no way he would give Rhiannon up now that he realized the odd sensations in his chest were love.

The woman wasn't to be found inside the great hall, and he assumed that was because she'd already been brought up to a chamber to bathe. So, he took the stairs two at a time, stopping outside each door, knocking and waiting for a response. When there was none, he continued up the circular stair until the distinct sounds of women laughing could be heard beyond a wooden door.

He knocked. The laughter stopped.

"My lady?" he said.

"Ian?" Douglass asked. "Rhiannon is indisposed at the moment."

"My goodness, brother, go away!" That was Matilda.

"I need to speak with her. 'Tis urgent."

"Are ye bleeding?" Iliana called through the door.

"This is highly inappropriate, and—" Whatever Douglass was going to continue saying, she stopped, and a second later, she opened the door, and three women (not including Rhiannon) glared at him. "I don't know what you think is so important, but apparently, she will listen."

Despite her tone and the glare, he detected the barest hint of a sparkle in her eyes, the same sparkle shared by his sisters.

Ian nodded. "I'll be quick." Though he didn't want to be.

Douglass nodded and stepped into the stairwell with Matilda and Iliana, the latter of whom pointed with two fingers at her eyes and then back at him. He grinned at her, grateful they'd allowed him a moment of privacy.

A screen was spread out in the center of the room, and beyond that, a few splashes were a subtle cue that Rhiannon was in the tub.

"Ian?" she called from behind the screen. "What is it?"

He drew in a breath, the fierce determination he'd had outside lodging somewhere in his throat. He'd never declared himself to a woman before, never felt this way about one either, and he was clueless about how to continue.

"I came here," he started and stopped.

"Aye?" More splashes.

"I wanted to say, before I head out to battle, that..." Why couldn't he seem to make his damn throat work? Every time he tried, he clammed up, and the pain in his chest only seemed to grow.

"Aye, Ian? What is it?" she pressed, though her voice was soft, concerned.

"I love ye." The words came out in a rush, and it wasn't even what he'd planned to say. But once they were out, he felt immensely lighter. And he knew them to be true. "I love ye so damn much."

There was a gasp, another splash and then silence.

My God, had he shocked her into a faint? Was she now drowning in the tub? He waited another beat, then started walking toward the screen when she appeared around the side of it, wrapped in a linen towel.

The sight of her took his breath. Her red-gold hair was damp and dripping sprinkles of bath water onto the floor. Her shoulders were sluiced with water, and the thin towel clung to her damp skin. Wide blue eyes stared up at him in wonder.

"You love me?" she asked.

"Aye. I've never loved another. And well…" He rubbed his hand over his heart and found that his words seemed lodged somewhere inside where his emotions were squeezing them.

"I've never loved another either, Ian."

Did that mean she loved him?

"I want ye to be my wife," he said, then rephrased. "That is if ye'll have me to be your husband."

Rhiannon grinned. "I would very much love to be your wife and to have you as a husband."

For the first time in his life, Ian's knees felt weak. He dropped to them on instinct before her, wrapping his arms around her hips and resting his head on her belly. Rhiannon rested her hand on his head, bending to kiss the top. They remained like that, silent, loving for several moments.

"When do you leave?" she asked.

Ian glanced up at her, not wanting to leave at all. "Soon as the men are ready."

"Marry me before you leave?" she said, shocking him and solidifying in him once more that they were meant to be, for wasn't that what he'd said outside?

"Noah is gathering Father August now."

"Get out," Douglass said, bursting through the door. "Out, out. If we're to have my dearest cousin ready to wed you, we cannot waste another minute with the two of you yammering on."

Ian leaped to his feet, staring at the three fierce women in the doorway.

Rhiannon laughed, and Ian hurried out of the chamber before they shoved him out. The door slammed behind him, and he hurried down the stairs to give his brother the good news.

Noah and Father August were standing in the great hall, talking quietly. The men had gathered too. Father August gave the men blessings before the battle, and while he was doing that, Ian told Noah she'd said aye.

"I knew ye had it in ye. Just needed to find the right woman."

"She suggested we wed before I went off into battle."

"As I said, the right woman."

Aye. A few moments later, the women returned, Rhiannon's wet hair pulled back into a plait, and a fresh gown clung to her curves. Ian was fairly certain he'd never seen her look more beautiful than she did at that moment, walking toward him to pledge herself to him as his wife for the rest of their days.

And he was confident the end of their days together wouldn't be today.

"My dear," Father August approached her. "I must take your confession first. And then yours." He pointed at Ian.

"I have committed no sin," Rhiannon said, "and I have prayed daily from the moment I left my brother's house until the last step into this room."

Ian forced himself not to smile at how pious she made herself appear, for they had sinned more than once on the journey to Castle Buanaiche, and he would have very much liked to have sinned when he saw her standing there in only the thin, wet linen from her bath.

"I, too, Father, confess that the only sin I have committed is wishing my enemies dead."

"Ye're absolved." Father August waved them forward and asked Rhiannon if she was there of her own free will.

"I am," she said, "but you may want to check on Laird Sinclair."

Ian swiveled his gaze toward her, shocked that she could be teasing a man of the cloth, but she looked entirely serious.

"Ian, are ye here of your own free will?" Father August asked, suddenly appearing very concerned.

Ian kept his laughter inside, realizing how serious Father August was. "I am indeed."

"Well, then we shall proceed. Do ye take each other to wed?"

"I do," they said at the same time.

"Then I declare ye man and wife." It was the quickest wedding ceremony Ian had ever witnessed. The hall erupted into cheers, and he took Rhiannon into his arms and kissed her as thoroughly as he'd wanted to upstairs.

When they finally broke apart, he stared into her eyes and whispered, "That will have to do until I return."

"I eagerly await the moment." She gripped him by the shirt, a slight tremble in her fingers, the teasing gone from her eyes. "Be careful. My brother doesn't fight fair, and I suspect the man he wanted me to marry won't either."

Ian put his hands over hers. "They willna beat me. Of that, I can promise."

And he meant it. Adam and his allies were going to rue the day they locked her up and then pursued her into Scotland.

As the men assembled outside, the women stood on the stairs, holding hands and watching.

"Adam is mine," Ian said to his brother. "I dinna want him killed."

"Did she ask that of ye?"

"Nay. But I'd hate for our wedding day to be marred by

the death of her one and only brother—even if he is an utter arse."

"Aye. Understood. We'll take him prisoner."

Ian nodded. "The other man, though, he can go to the devil."

Noah grinned. "My favorite place to send men of that sort."

The Sinclair army mounted their horses, armed with their swords, daggers, battle axes and targes, and signaled for the gates to be opened.

It was time to make their enemies pay.

⚜

IT WAS A GOOD THING THAT DOUGLASS HELD HER HAND because Rhiannon was ready to dart from where she stood on the steps into the sea of armed men on horseback and grab Ian. To tell him that maybe it wasn't worth it. Perhaps they should negotiate.

But she knew that wouldn't work. Not with Adam nor his gambling cohort. Neither of those men were willing to give her up. They'd risked bringing an army to the northern Highlands to prove that point. They weren't going to say, "All right then, let us negotiate."

"They will return." Douglass sounded so calm and confident that Rhiannon tried to do the same.

She straightened her shoulders. "Of course, they will."

"Would you like us to go to the ramparts?"

"Oh, thank heavens." Rhiannon let out a long sigh. "I thought you'd never ask."

Douglass grinned. "I have to do it every time Noah leaves."

They made their way up to the ramparts, where Matilda and Iliana were already waiting, the two staring over the side as the sea of warriors left the castle to meet the army assembled on the horizon.

"Bastards were already waiting for them," Iliana said.

"Bastards, indeed," Rhiannon murmured.

They watched the men until they came to a stop. Their shouts back and forth carried on the wind, but not the actual words, leaving the women to use their imaginations on what was being said.

"Will your brother surrender if he knows Ian has wed ye?" Matilda asked.

"Nay," Rhiannon and Douglass said at the same time.

"If anything, that will only enrage him," Rhiannon said. "He's pledged me to the other bastard down there to pay off a debt. Me being already wed means that he won't be able to pay off that debt."

"Ah, so either way, your brother will have to fight."

"Aye."

"And I assume he will hope to make ye a widow this day and cart ye off," Iliana said.

"Likely so." Rhiannon's tone was filled with all the sadness she felt in her heart.

If only Adam had ever cared about her, maybe they wouldn't be in this situation. But perhaps that wasn't the issue. He was a gambler, and gambling men had debts. Gambling men were threatened with their lives, and they often became desperate. And desperate men did stupid things.

This was a stupid thing, for it was certain death for him at the hands of the Scots.

From all the shouting back and forth, it was evident the men were attempting to negotiate, and Rhiannon had to hand it to Ian for at least trying. He really did love her, didn't he?

But the shouting stopped, and those sent forward to

negotiate returned to their places in line with their men, and her heart stuttered to a halt.

A loud horn sounded from one of the Scots—the call for the battle to begin. The sound was chilling, and goose flesh rose on her bones; her heart, finally figuring out how to beat, thundered behind her ribs.

"I don't know if I can watch," she said.

"Turn around," Douglass said. "If you go down the stairs, you'll only come up again."

Rhiannon nodded, but her feet stilled even as she started to turn. The men raised their swords and targes in the air. The English raised their weapons, and battle cries sounded from both, reverberating back against the stones and vibrating in her ears.

For a second, Rhiannon closed her eyes. Let the sounds fade. Pretended she was back on the road with Ian. That nothing was happening. Just the two of them smiling, laughing.

Goosie took that moment to appear, winding her way around Rhiannon's legs. Rhiannon lifted her cat, pressing her face into Goosie's neck, and felt some semblance of peace. She faced the deafening battle, the clash of swords and bellows, knowing that it wouldn't last long, and soon Ian would return to her.

❧ 16 ❧

Ian loved a challenge.

He was always the first to step up when a challenge was laid out before him. And nothing about that had changed.

Except this time, facing the enemy on a field of battle felt different. *He* was different.

Only an invisible line separated him from his foe. The usual rush of fire buzzed through his veins—battle lust—but tucked into that rush was something else. Something deeper. A need to protect what was his. The woman he loved. The life they'd only recently discovered they were meant to live—together.

Ian didn't turn around.

Because if he took one look at his wife up on the battlements—his *wife*—he might go berserk and annihilate every damned one of the *Sassenachs* jeering before him.

And a warrior was no good to anyone in that kind of state. He might as well sign his own death warrant if he did that. Battle was not a place one should lose control.

And so, he braced himself, ground his teeth, and flexed

his fingers against the hilt of his sword and the strap of his horse's reins. The targe on his arm was a welcome weight.

"The battle is yours to call," Noah said, "But do ye want to try to negotiate first?"

Bloody hell nay, Ian wanted to shout. He wanted to cut these men down where they stood. It was only because he respected his wife that he wouldn't kill her brother for bringing danger to them all.

As much as he wanted to wreak havoc on the bastards, he also knew it would be better to have at least tried negotiating before any blood was drawn. That way, he could look his wife in the eyes when he told her he'd vanquished the men who sought to take her, and she could look back at him with respect.

"I'll go with ye." Noah sheathed his sword and gave Ian a look that said, "Sheath your damn sword, brother."

Begrudgingly, Ian followed Noah's lead and put his sword away, feeling the emptiness in his hand as if he'd removed an appendage.

"Ready?"

"Nay." Ian drew in a breath, trying to quell the rage that threatened to take hold of him. "But I will be."

Noah nodded, and the two of them dismounted and walked steadily forward, approaching the blasted *Sassenachs* who sat on their horses and stared down their noses at them as if they owned this land and would take what they wanted from it. The same attitude that had been going on for decades.

"Get off your horse and negotiate," Ian shouted up at the man in the middle. He instinctively knew this was Rhiannon's brother. It wasn't so much that he looked like her, but something about the shape of the nose and the mouth was familiar. Though where her expression was often teasing, Adam's was arrogant.

"You deign to tell me what to do?" the man sneered down at him, then spit on the ground.

Ian bristled, and it took everything inside him not to wrench the bloody foking arse off his horse and pummel him into the ground.

"I dinna deign to do anything but kick your arse, but I'm trying to be a gentleman about it," Ian spoke through gritted teeth, his hands flexing at his sides and itching to wipe this blight from the earth. "For Lady Rhiannon's sake."

"You, a gentleman?" Adam scoffed. "You stole my sister from my lands. You abducted her like the bloody heathen you are. Likely ravaged her, and now you're holding her carcass for ransom."

What the hell? Adam was insane. Rude, mad and an idiot.

Ian scowled up at his brother-by-marriage—even thinking of him in those terms turned his stomach. "Your sister is on the battlements watching ye right now, alive and well, no' a carcass. And I didna need to steal her from your lands, for she asked me to take her. And a real man does no' need to rape his woman."

Adam bristled. "She's *not* yours. Rhiannon is already spoken for."

Ian shook his head, locking eyes in a deadly stare. "Ye're right about one thing—she is spoken for. She's my wife, and I'll no' let ye have her."

"Your...*wife!*" Adam went nearly purple in the face, spittle flying as he said it.

The man seated on the horse beside him, who Ian took to be the very one who thought he'd spoken for Rhiannon, glared daggers at essentially everything and everyone.

Adam stared over Ian's head, likely toward the battlements where Rhiannon was standing, not that Ian had looked. He still couldn't. But he could feel her presence there, and that was enough to scare the wits out of him.

"How dare you marry my betrothed," the other man said.

"How dare you buy her from her brother," Ian retorted. "Did anyone never teach ye that people should not be bought and sold?"

"Buy? That is not how it works," the man seethed. "We had a contract, an agreement." He over-pronounced each *T* as if Ian didn't understand the language.

Ian shrugged because he didn't give a damn. "That was how it worked for ye. Adam owed ye a debt; ye tried to take payment in the form of his sister."

"How dare you call me Adam!" his brother-by-marriage shouted in outrage.

Ian was growing bored with this ridiculous back and forth. This was not a negotiation, but more like a few green lads pissing on each other in the bailey after lessons. "Is that no' your name?"

"No heathen should dare say it."

"If ye're referring to me as the heathen, then I just did." Ian couldn't help goading him, and he got great satisfaction from the fury pouring from Adam.

"I ought to beat you for speaking to me with such insolence," Adam hissed.

"Come down off your horse. I'd be happy to let ye try." Ian held his hands to the side, challenging the idiot to do that. What he wouldn't give to let him have a few swipes and then pummel his idiotic arse into the ground.

"The insolence!"

Ian rolled his eyes and glanced at Noah, who seemed to be enjoying the show.

"Are ye willing to negotiate?" Ian asked. "Or shall we fight? The choice is yours, but I willna offer it more than once."

"We do not negotiate with heathens."

"A fight, then."

"To the death!" Rhiannon's brother pulled his sword, and his friend beside him did the same.

"If ye say so." Ian shook his head and looked at Noah who held a similar expression. They headed back to their horses. "This is no' going to be a fair fight."

"No," Noah said.

"I dinna want to kill her brother. Everyone else is fair game."

"What do ye intend to do with him?" Noah and Ian mounted their horses, gazes on the men who'd come to fight.

"I think, take him prisoner for now. Perhaps I'll let my wife decide what we do with him. We could always take him back to Orkney, and he'd have no way to escape unless he stole a ship, which seems unlikely."

Noah chuckled. "The man would go mad."

"Perhaps it will cure him of what ails him."

"Gambling problem?"

"Aye. Can ye imagine gambling away one of our sisters?"

"No' for the life of me. Besides, Iliana would kill us in our sleep if we tried."

"Verra true. Shall we get on with this?"

"I think it best. I'm hungry."

Ian nodded to the man down the line, who lifted the Sinclair battle horn to his lips and let out a mighty blow. The sound of it sent a rush through Ian every time. The men were trained to fight at that sound. The intensity of it was like a switch in their brains.

Ian raised his sword over his head and let out a mighty bellow that Noah and the rest of the Sinclair warriors echoed.

Before them, Rhiannon's brother, his friend and their men all looked startled by the show of intensity. They had no idea what they were getting into, which seemed unfair, but Ian had given them a way out. Pride controlled them all. None wanted to give up what they'd spent days searching for.

And none of them were honest enough with themselves to acknowledge defeat when it stood before them or rather rode, sword drawn and filled with blood lust.

Ian gave the signal, and his men rushed forward.

Adam, not surprisingly, rode his horse to the back of his army. His friend didn't notice until it was too late and was forced to engage.

Ian made slow, methodical work of the men before him, knocking them out rather than killing them when he could. He kept his gaze on Adam the entire time. Let the wee man believe he was about to be hacked down. Inciting fear was half the effort, wasn't it?

A fitting punishment for a boorish brother who thought he could rule his sister and force her into marriage.

But Adam didn't seem to have the guts to stick around. And before Ian had gotten through Adam's men, the coward turned his horse around and started to run.

"Och, nay, ye bastard," Ian ground out.

He urged his mount into a gallop, racing through the English soldiers who half-heartedly attempted to stop him. Ian broke through the melee, the heels of his boots pressing into his horse's flank, urging him to go faster.

Adam kept turning his head around, seeing Ian following and screeching words lost on the wind, but probably as cowardly as running away.

Fortunately, or unfortunately, he wasn't paying attention and steered his horse right into a tree. The horse halted abruptly, causing Adam sail over the neck of his mount and hit his head with a mighty smack into the trunk. But his feet were caught in the stirrups, yanking him back down, where he slumped on the horse.

"Oh, for the love of..." Ian grumbled.

He reached Adam's horse. Adam's body hunched over,

unconscious, with a massive gash on his forehead that bled with the force of a waterfall after a heavy rain.

Ian knew from experience that head wounds often bled like that. And that they looked worse than they were; however, the idiot had hit the tree quite hard, and it was possible he'd cracked his skull.

With a sigh, Ian yanked the man off his horse and over his lap. He wrapped his bleeding head in a torn piece of Adam's shirt, and then headed back toward the castle, unsurprised to see that the battle had been quelled. A few English lay on the ground. The rest galloped away, having surrendered no doubt.

"Hit his head on a tree."

"I suppose that's one way to decide your fate," Noah said with a shake of his head.

"The fool." Ian glanced up at the castle battlements where Rhiannon was watching. "At least it wasna my doing. I'm no' certain I could have faced her if I'd been the one to crush his skull."

"Is he still alive?"

Ian glanced down. "A little."

"Best to get him seen by our healer then."

"Aye. What happened to his friend?"

"Ran off with his army."

"Hopefully for good."

"Aye."

Noah gave orders for the few bodies to be buried. They'd taken it quite easy on the ill-prepared army. Ian went through the opened gates in search of the healer.

Rhiannon met him inside the bailey, her somber eyes on her brother's body.

"He should have been paying attention," she said.

"He should no' have run. I wasna going to harm him...much."

"He's a coward." She shrugged. "Cowards run."

"So did his friend. Shame. Would ye like to come with me to see him to the healer?"

"Aye."

Ian dismounted, and carried her brother's limp body inside the castle, where a healer was already waiting in the great hall. Every battle, they prepared for such occasions, even when the battles seemed like an easy win. One wrong move in the wrong direction could mean life or death. Thus far, Ian and his brothers had been lucky, but there would come a day when their bodies aged losing the ability to be as fluid and in control as they were now, and when it came, he would risk death.

Ian laid Adam on the table that had been prepared for the wounded. The healer removed the hastily tied wrap Ian had put in place, revealing a mighty gash in the center of Adam's forehead that pulsed blood at a rather steady pace, though slower than the geyser of when it first happened.

"Good sign," the healer said. "A pulsing wound means he's still alive."

Ian nodded, and Rhiannon relaxed beside him. She might have hated her brother for what he had done to her, but that didn't mean she wished him dead. Ian knew that. It was the reason he hadn't planned to kill the man. Why did Adam, the bloody fool, have to run?

Wanting to comfort his wife, Ian tucked his arm around her and pulled her closer. Rhiannon leaned against him, her head on his shoulder, her body sinking into his.

They watched together as the healer poked and prodded at the wound and then proceeded to wash it, pulled a chip of bark out. Adam moaned as the healer worked but didn't open his eyes or appear to regain consciousness.

After cleaning out the wound, the healer sewed him up and then put a salve on the wound. By now, the bleeding had stopped, and by the time his head was wrapped, he mostly looked as if he were sleeping, save for the extremely pale coloring of his cheeks.

"Just need to watch out for fever now," the healer said, pouring a tincture into Adam's mouth that he choked and sputtered on but which the healer coaxed him to swallow with a few massages to his throat. "That ought to help and keep him asleep. We'll give him this," she wiggled the bottle, "every few hours."

"Thank you," Rhiannon said.

The healer nodded. "If he can beat the fever, he'll likely live. Canna say if he'll wake the same way he was before the injury. Some men with head wounds like that come back a wee bit daft. Only time will tell."

Rhiannon nodded, and Ian grimaced. If the man came back daft, he'd be their responsibility for the rest of his life, and while Ian had planned to keep Adam prisoner for a little while, he'd also planned on sending the idiot back to England with a warning never to set foot in Scotland again. Now, it seemed that was not going to be an option.

"We'll pray he heals," Rhiannon said.

"Aye, and perhaps give a few tithes." Ian glanced up at the rafters of the great hall, speaking to the heavens in silence that he would promise whatever it took to get this man healed and back to his own lands.

Ian took Rhiannon's hand and led her away from the healer, who was now tending a few warriors with minor injuries.

"May I get ye some wine?" he asked, knowing it would help heal her nerves a little bit.

"Nay. No wine."

"Is there anything I can do?"

She shook her head and walked toward the hearth.

Ian followed.

"You were fearless out there," she said.

"No' without some fear."

She glanced up at him. "No one would believe that."

He grinned. "We're supposed to look terrifying to our enemies."

"You did."

"And were ye scared...of me?"

She shook her head. "Not at all. Mostly, I was worried my brother would be reckless. That he'd direct all of his men to kill just you, and you'd have a pile of them on you."

"They'd never have made it that far."

"Aye, I figured that out relatively quickly."

"I didna plan to harm your brother," he said, needing to tell her this. "I wanted to take him prisoner. I gave the order. But he ran."

She nodded. "I appreciate that. I would have never asked."

"Ye could have. Ye can always ask. I respect ye, Rhiannon. And I want our marriage to be a partnership, one where we can speak about such things. I'm no' a brute."

She grinned at him, taking his hand in hers. "I've never thought you were a brute. And I appreciate you wanting my opinion."

"It's only fair. Why should I be the only one making decisions?"

"It is traditional for the husband to do so." She shrugged.

"Aye, and if either of us followed traditions, ye'd be married to the man who's run off with your brother's army."

Rhiannon shuddered. "Then I am glad that we both are rebels."

🦋 17 🦋

With the great hall cleared of patients and Rhiannon's brother tucked into a chamber to heal—with guards outside the door—the clan prepared for a festive celebration.

Hours ago, the great hall had been a somber place; to look at it now, Rhiannon might have been in a different castle.

Fresh flowers had been brought in, brightening the space. Herbed rushes were replaced on the floor with new ones. A piper was playing a spirited tune with a fiddler, and a woman was playing the fife.

The music filled the hall, and people were smiling and dancing. Noah and Douglass sat on the dais, but Iliana and Matilda were in the center of the dancing, and surprisingly, so was Ian. He tugged her into the throng and swung her about. She was shocked after the battle that the men had enough energy to do more than imbibe ale.

From the emotional toll of it all, she'd felt like doing nothing more than flopping into a chair and napping for maybe a week. But their energy was contagious, so she joined the dance with exuberance.

As Ian swung her, her chest filled with a feeling that was hard to describe. Longing and happiness all at once. Somehow, in the last few weeks she'd known him, she'd fallen desperately in love with Ian. The fact that he was now her husband was surreal.

She was a Sinclair.

These people were now her people. And Douglass, her beautiful cousin, was her cousin now twice over.

She glanced toward the dais where Noah had his hand on Douglass's belly and whispered something in her ear. They were so in love, and the vision of the two of them was incredibly endearing.

Ian twirled her in another circle, bending her over his arm, his eyes on hers, the smile on his face so pure she could melt from seeing it.

"I love ye, lass," he said.

Tears of joy filled Rhiannon's eyes. "Oh, Ian, I love you so very much."

He lifted her back up and kissed her right there in front of everyone until all sense and breath left her.

Cheers rang out from the clansmen and women. Feet thundered on the wooden floorboards, and hands clapped. They called out for Ian to kiss her again, and before she had a chance to process, he was wrapping her in his arms and making the world melt away all over again.

This was what it was like to be loved, to be cherished.

There had been moments when they were on their way to Scotland that she'd worried she might not be accepted. She had no idea where she'd fit in. After all, she was English and begging charity from her English cousin, who happened to be married to a laird. What if people didn't want yet another Englishwoman amongst them?

But she'd not counted on falling in love. She'd not counted on Ian.

Rhiannon felt so blessed in this moment, her heart thudding hard against her ribs and a smile so wide on her face, she was sure her cheeks would ache in the morning. This might be the happiest day of her life. Which also made her feel a little guilty, given her brother was lying upstairs sleeping the sleep of the injured, with a healer making sure he didn't succumb to a fever.

Besides that part, she would change nothing of this moment—until Ian gave her a look that made her toes curl.

"I want to take ye to bed," he whispered in her ear.

She nodded, swallowing, warmth and heady anticipation encasing her.

Ian gripped her hand in his and tugged her toward the stairs. The loud shouts from the great hall were as deafening as they were when he kissed her. But she didn't care. Being led by Ian was what she wanted to be for the rest of her days. A safe haven. A loving one.

He had delivered her from a dismal future she couldn't even contemplate, and now here they were, *married*. For the rest of their lives, she'd be by his side. Ian swept her into his arms and climbed at a pace that made her cling to him.

When they reached the chamber they'd share for the night, he shut the door behind them but still held her close.

"You can put me down," she teased. And yet, her arms tightened around his shoulders as she said it as if her body didn't want to let go.

Ian pressed his forehead to hers and whispered, "What if I never want to let ye go?"

Rhiannon kissed his lips lightly, emotion swelling her chest. "I would hold on."

"Och, lass, that is exactly what I want to hear. I never thought I'd get married, and now I canna fathom no' being your husband. No' having ye as my wife."

Husband.

Aye, hers. All hers.

When she was a girl, Rhiannon dreamed of being a wife one day. But as the years went on, she hadn't been so certain. And then, when her brother came along, the idea had been abhorrent. Not in her wildest dreams had she ever believed she'd have a husband who thrilled her with a look.

A husband she loved.

Ian's lips brushed lightly over hers, and Rhiannon lost her train of thought. She let all the worries, the angst, the horrors of the past fall away.

"I love ye, lass. I think I fell in love with ye the moment I first spied ye and Goosie in the wood."

Rhiannon bit her lip, her belly flipping as happiness flooded her. "I'll be forever grateful you came for me, Ian. You risked so much crossing the border for a stranger." Rhiannon cupped his cheek, loving the way his stubble tickled her palm. "I love you so much. You make me feel so warm, safe, and cherished." Emotion ran wild inside her, threatening to spill over into tears, so she smiled and teased, "And who could not love a man who rides a horse with a cat tucked into his shirt?"

Ian chuckled. "Goosie has my heart, too, lass."

"She's a lucky cat. And I'm a lucky woman."

"Och, the luck is all mine."

With her arms wrapped around his shoulders, Rhiannon pressed her lips to his, desiring nothing more than to be intoxicated by her husband's kiss. He tasted of the whiskey he'd sipped during the feast and as sweet as the spiced fruit pies they'd been served after they supped.

Ian's tongue slid over hers in slow, tantalizing swipes, causing tingles to skate along her flesh, hardening her nipples, settling in her core, and making her quiver.

Ian carried her to the massive four-poster bed. The Sinclair plaid curtains were already tugged open, and the bedclothes turned down in anticipation of their arrival. He laid her down, then just as swiftly was beside her.

As soon as they hit the mattress, excitement and feral memory overcame her. Oh, how she'd wanted to make love to him.

Ian kissed her gently, stroking her softly on her arms and the nape of her neck until her body trembled with need. He slid his mouth along her throat and up to her ear. "I want ye so bad I can taste it."

Rhiannon tilted her head to the side, allowing him better access. "I want you to taste me."

Her thoughts had turned carnal, lusty, as she imagined him gliding his muscular form over her, his tongue swirling and dipping.

Ian laughed softly, a delicious gravelly sound.

With every breath, every kiss, shivers glided over her limbs, firing like arrows from a thousand bows.

Ian kissed her softly, then urged her to sit up. "I need to get ye out of this dress. I want to feel your skin. All of ye."

Rhiannon nodded and lifted on her knees, turning around for him to unlace her gown. Guiding her hands to the headboard to hold on as she knelt on the bed, and he moved behind her. With nimble fingers, he unlaced her, following the removal of each piece of clothing with a soft kiss on her exposed skin. He unlaced her boots and unrolled her hose, tickling the arch of her feet. When he was done, his coarse hands spanned her waist, stroking her flesh.

"I love your skin. It's so soft," he whispered against her throat.

Rhiannon sighed, every part of her shivering with excitement. A twinge of some deeper, delicious sensation clutched at her core. A desire to be with him, to feel his sensual touch.

Rhiannon clutched the headboard while Ian explored her naked back with his fingers and lips. He slid a path down her spine to the place at the top of her buttocks, and she sucked in a breath. Coarse palms cupped the globes of her bottom, massaging, and she bit her lip as pleasure coursed through her.

"Stunning." His mouth followed the path of her spine until he reached her neck, then turned her chin slightly to capture her lips in a searing kiss.

Rhiannon gave him all of herself, whimpering when he caressed the sides of her breasts. Her nipples were taut, tingling knots. A primal hunger took hold, moving her body in ways she couldn't have conjured in her wildest dreams. Her hips pushed back, seeking the hardness of his body, the thickness of his arousal. The bare skin of her buttocks met the scratchy wool of his plaid. She wanted him to be rid of his clothes too.

Rhiannon turned around, wrapping her arms around Ian's neck and kissed him deeply, hungrily. "Ye're still dressed," she teased, plucking at his plaid.

Ian unpinned his plaid, letting the fabric fall from his shoulder. Then he crossed his arms over his middle and lifted his *leine* over his head, revealing inch after inch of muscle and sinew.

Rhiannon reached for him. Touching, exploring as he'd done to her, marveling at the contrast of their skin. She slid her palms over his chest with the soft sprinkle of hair, down his abdomen to the line of hair trailing beneath his plaid. She hooked a finger around his belt but then froze as his touch traced along her belly and lower.

Rhiannon's head fell back as the pads of Ian's fingers slipped over her slickened folds, finding the knot of flesh. He rubbed in delicious circles, sending heady ripples through her center.

She wobbled on her knees, clutching at his shoulders for balance.

"Lie down."

Rhiannon did as he demanded, watching as Ian undid his belt, pulling off his plaid.

Rhiannon licked her lips at the sight of his arousal. Long. Thick. Hard. It jutted from between his hips, reaching for her, and she wanted very much to accept the invitation.

"I want to...touch you," she said.

Ian's smile was wolfish, and her head felt fuzzy with desire. He gripped her hand and tugged it toward his arousal, her fingers brushing the velvet tip. He shuddered, pleasure washing over his handsome features as she stroked him.

Rhiannon explored further, admiring that he was both hard and soft at the same time. Caressing up and down his length, she wrapped her fingers around the shaft and gave a little tug.

Her husband grabbed her hand, a groan on his lips. "No more."

"You don't like it?"

"I like it too much." And then he was kissing her, rubbing between her legs with his expert touch until she was gasping and losing all thought.

He traced a line down her neck to her breasts with his tongue, swirling the tip around one nipple until she groaned and dug her nails into his bare shoulder. He continued to work his fingers between her legs, rubbing, pushing inside her, until she was writhing, clutching him, her hips undulating in rhythm with his taunting, until pleasure gripped her in a climax.

"Ian!" she cried out, panting in delight.

"Och, lass, I love the way ye come undone with my touch."

Ian slid down her body, pushing apart her knees. Her thighs still trembled from her release, and she watched the hungry expression on his face as he spied her most sensitive, secret place. And then he lowered himself and licked her. *There*.

Rhiannon cried out with pleasure once more, her back arching, hips rising to meet the languid strokes of his tongue. Lovemaking was so decadent.

The more his tongue licked with wicked purpose over her heated flesh, the more she fell apart and the harder it was to breathe.

When her body peaked once more, she squeezed her thighs against his head, her fingers diving into his hair.

"My, oh my, you are good at that."

Ian winked, a satisfied grin on his full lips. "A man could never hear better words spoken."

Ian slid up the length of her body, his arousal pressing against her still-quivering folds. "Now, to make ye mine, all over again."

Their gazes locked, a powerful and intoxicating passion passing between them.

"I love you," she said.

"I love ye with every breath and beat of my heart." And then he was kissing her again, drowning her in desire and pleasure.

When he parted her folds and notched his arousal at her center. He murmured that it may hurt, but she lifted her hips, urging him to drive inside. They both moaned as he filled her, stretching her, the tiniest pinch of pain was there and then gone, erased by his kiss.

Ian shuddered over her, his forehead falling to hers, as he placed tiny kiss after kiss on her mouth, and then deeper as he slid out and slowly pushed back in.

"Wrap your legs around me."

Rhiannon submitted, gasping at how wrapping her legs around his hips deepened his thrusts.

Their kiss turned frenzied, each demanding more with

the slide of their tongues and nibbling lips. Making love to Ian was heaven on earth.

He withdrew and thrust deeper and deeper and deeper still. Rhiannon met each thrust with the rise of her hips.

"I am the luckiest man in Scotland." Ian kissed her deeply in a kiss that felt as if he were claiming her soul.

Rhiannon clung to him, kissing him back as passionately. This man was hers and hers alone until the end of time. "I am the luckiest woman."

Their bodies crashed together on the shores of pleasure, sweet, delicious release rolling them in wave upon wave as they clung to each other as if they were each the other's life line.

When their shudders subsided, Ian rolled to his side, pulling her along his length. He tucked her in his embrace and kissed her lovingly on the temple. "I'm glad ye're mine."

"Nothing will come between us ever again."

❧ 18 ❧

The last time Ian had left the Orkney shores and his castle, Balla Dorcha, he'd not expected to return with anyone, let alone a wife. And yet there, standing on the bow of his ship with him, the wind blowing her hair around her face, was Rhiannon, the new Lady of Orkney.

Mistress of Balla Dorcha.

He was still mesmerized every time he looked at her. There was a permanent lift to the corner of his mouth. They'd been wed a week now—of which they'd remained at Buanaiche, awaiting her brother's ability to ride and, of course, allowing Rhiannon and Douglass to spend time together since they hadn't seen each other in so long.

The days were filled with games and chatter, and the nights after feasting were spent in hours of endless pleasure. When it had come time to leave, Rhiannon looked sadly upon her cousin, who was ready to give birth in the next month. Noah had promised to send word when she went into labor, and Ian had promised to make certain Rhiannon was there in time to help.

Only a month had passed since he'd first come upon Rhiannon at the edge of the wood in England. And yet, in that short amount of time, so much had changed for him.

Ian saw life with new eyes. The world itself held a new meaning.

He stroked his hand over Goosie's head and back where the cat perched on the ship's rail, looking stoically out to sea and perhaps contemplating why her humans would have forced her to travel over water.

"I can't wait to see your home," Rhiannon said.

"It's never really been a home to me. More like...a stronghold." He cringed at how cold that sounded.

"Stronghold?" She raised a brow at him.

"Aye. I grew up with my brothers at Castle Buanaiche. It wasn't until I came of age that I was sent to Balla Dorcha to take my seat and place as Earl of Orkney. I think that's why I'm always drawn back to Noah's holding—that is home."

She looked at him, perplexed. "I don't think I knew you were an earl. I guess that makes me a countess." She started to laugh.

Ian chuckled right along with her. "Aye. I suppose I've never thought of myself as an earl."

"And now?"

"So much has changed." He slung his arm around her shoulders and tugged her close, kissing her on her temple. "For the better."

The sailing from Noah's shores to his own was swift, and when they disembarked, Ian's men escorted Adam off the ship and to his new quarters. The man was belligerent, his words still a little slurred from the heavy amounts of spirits they'd been giving him to keep him mildly subdued. The bandage was no longer wrapped around his head, and the place he'd knocked into the tree now had a wicked red, stitched wound.

Despite being tired, he seemed otherwise to be all right. No lasting damage to his brain.

Adam did try to say when he first woke that it had been Ian's fault he was injured. However, Ian and several witnesses to his accident were quick to point out that, no, indeed, Adam only had himself to blame.

Adam seemed to have blocked out his riding away from the fray, the abandonment of his men. Running smack into a tree when he wasn't looking. The only thing he was grateful for regarding the mishap was that his horse wasn't injured.

What the English prig did remember clearly was that Rhiannon had betrayed him. She'd rolled her eyes and told him how ironic that was coming out of his mouth after he had sold her to his friend.

"How long will you keep him?" Rhiannon smoothed her skirts at the base of the gangway as Adam hollered about his treatment while he passed them by. So much for spirits subduing him.

"Until I'm certain he does no' plan to return to Scotland to wreak more havoc."

"Ah. That seems as if it will be a long time coming then." Rhiannon laughed. "Seems that is all my brother knows how to do."

"Likely. I'll give him a fortnight before the servants start making plans to ship him off to France."

Rhiannon let out a sigh. "Might we send him back sooner? Mayhap his friend can deal with him."

"That might be a death sentence." He meant it as a joke, but the moment the words were out of his mouth, he knew the truth in them.

Rhiannon grimaced. This was a conversation they'd had before. She wanted her brother to suffer a little after he'd imprisoned her in their castle, but at the same time, she didn't have the heart for vengeance. And he didn't either. The man was a bastard, but that didn't mean he deserved to die. The self-inflicted head wound was enough.

"I do hope he doesn't put a damper on our newly wedded lives." She frowned, watching him as he kicked and wriggled against the hold of the Sinclair men.

"Dinna fash, love. I've made sure he'll be someplace we canna hear him."

"The dungeon?" She glanced up at him, her mouth forming an *O* of surprise.

"Nay, lass, no' the dungeon. He'd hardly survive a day, let alone as many as he needs. The rats would eat him alive if madness didna take him first. Just a room no' near our own."

"There is a lot of truth in those words." She let out a sigh and pushed her hair out of her face. "He's been coddled his whole life and gotten everything he wanted."

"Aye, and we must remember that he put himself in this position in more ways than one."

Rhiannon slid her arm around his and leaned against him, enveloping him in her floral scent. "And if he had not, we never would have met."

"I dinna think that's true. We would have met eventually, and I'd have still been a bachelor. I would have been immediately captivated by your charm, and the rest would be the same as now—minus the arsehole brother."

She glanced up at him, all seriousness in her gaze. "Ah, things may have remained the same for you, but I might have been wed." She pressed her lips together, obviously trying not to laugh.

"Dinna say such things," he teased. "I would have murdered your husband, tossed ye over my shoulder and claimed ye as my own. That would have left a lasting impression."

"Oh, it most certainly would."

"But not the kind I'd need to be certain ye'd wed me after we buried him."

Rhiannon laughed. "I might have been persuaded to come around. And you'd be lucky not to bear the brunt of my dagger if I had."

"I will bear any injury ye believe I deserve." Ian tilted her chin and kissed her briefly on the lips. "Welcome to Orkney, Countess."

Ian's chest swelled as his people swarmed from within the castle walls to greet them near the dock. They all looked on Rhiannon with surprise and joy. Several even pulled her in for a hug.

"My laird, we're so glad ye've returned." Mac, his seneschal, embraced Ian in a hearty hug.

"'Tis been too long," Ian said, clapping his friend on the back. "How goes it here?"

"All is well, my laird. About a month ago, there was a ship-wreck nearby." He pointed toward the west of the isle, where debris from ships lost at sea often washed up. "We were able to save a few people, but the rest perished."

Ian and Rhiannon crossed themselves, praying for those who'd been lost.

"And the few ye saved?" Ian asked.

Mac smiled. "Hale and hearty now. Helping out with clan duties until their ship is repaired, though it is no' looking good. The damage is quite extensive. Might be best to simply sail them home ourselves."

"Where did they come from?" Rhiannon asked.

"Ireland. We get a lot of those, believe it or not," Mac said.

"Ah. Then we'd best get them where they want to be," Ian said.

Mac's eyes widened for a moment, a look of yearning on his face, held long enough that Ian could see his seneschal longed to escape the isles, too, if only for a wee adventure. The man had damned well earned it.

"How about ye captain that voyage?" Ian offered.

Mac looked up sharply. "What about Balla Dorcha?"

Ian glanced toward Rhiannon, who was kneeling and speaking to a child holding out a bouquet.

"I'm going to remain on the isle a while with my wife."

Mac grinned. "Never thought we'd see the day."

Ian chuckled. "Neither did I, but here I am. And ye gods, am I happy."

Mac pounded him on the back, his smile wide. "Glad we are, my laird, glad we are."

Ian and Rhiannon moved slowly through the crowd, with Ian in no hurry, wanting to pay attention to his people and introduce his wife. At last, they were walking through the gates of his thick stone walls and up the stone steps to the keep. Before, it had felt like a stronghold, but now, with Rhiannon by his side with a future to plan for, this place felt like a lot more.

It almost felt like home.

"Your clan is so welcoming," she said.

"They are truly remarkable people."

"I can see why you're proud of them. And the isle."

"I want to show ye." He led her back down the stairs, then another set of stairs that led up to the battlements.

At the top, they could walk the perimeter and see the sea in the front and the rest of the isle at the back. His village surrounded the castle, and the fields beyond were dotted with sheep and cows.

"Magnificent," Rhiannon breathed.

"It is a verra peaceful place."

Her hand slipped into his. "And you think you'll be able to remain for a little while? I heard you tell Mac he could make the voyage to Ireland."

"Aye. For ye." Ian turned to her, cupping her face as he kissed her. "I want to make a life with ye. And I think this is a good place to start."

"I'm excited for this life together."

An irritated meow at their legs had them both laughing.

"I'm not sure Goosie is as excited as we are."

"She will be soon. There's nowhere her prey can run, and they won't swim back to the mainland."

Rhiannon laughed, the sound like magic stardust to his soul.

"Come, I want to show ye the rest of the keep."

They entered the great hall where servants were bustling to set the table, chattering excitedly.

"My laird." Cook rushed up to them, his cheeks rosy and a grin of merriment reaching his eyes. "I'm preparing your favorite meal." Then he looked worried. "At least I hope it's still your favorite meal."

"All meals are my favorite," Ian declared, squeezing the man's shoulder.

"Excellent, my laird." Then, seeming to realize who he was standing in front of, Cook bowed to Rhiannon, "My lady, I do hope ye like pheasant pie."

"I'm certain I will love it, Cook."

After showing her the other chambers in the keep, Ian finally showed her the bedchamber they would share. As he pushed through the door, watching her eyes scan every part, it was as if he were seeing it through her eyes for the first time.

The stone walls, wide wood floor planks. The massive bed in the center was not the typical four-poster with curtains but intimidating all the same. The headboard and footboards were made from the doors of the enemy holdings he'd vanquished, with the metal rings of their ring-pulls still in the center of the intricately carved Celtic knots. A chest at the foot of the bed held extra blankets and the wardrobe beside it had his clothes. On the wall above the bed were wide circular shields with ancient runes, swords, lances and axes.

It was a warrior's chamber, and he worried she'd see it as that. A brutal reminder of the life he'd led. But instead, she turned and smiled.

"This room is a glimpse into your soul, isn't it?"

Ian grunted a laugh. "I suppose it is. We can take down some of the weapons if ye like?"

"Oh, no, I wouldn't dare do such a thing. Besides, if the castle is besieged at night, we can grab a sword from the wall and push back the enemy."

"Ye know how to use a sword?"

She shrugged. "A dagger, aye, as you've seen. With a sword, I'm merely passing. But I want to learn. And shouldn't the Countess of Orkney know how to protect her lands as well as her husband? Or at least almost as well?"

"I will protect ye always, my love." Ian put his arms around her and pulled her into his embrace, kissing her gently on the lips.

"I have no doubt you will. But it would be silly for us to think that you won't be called away."

"I'll take you with me."

"There may be times I can't go." She bit her lip and glanced toward the bed. "If I am with child or have just delivered one."

He nodded, not having thought about that before. "I will do whatever it is ye wish. If it's swords ye wish to learn, I will teach ye. I already know ye can ride like the wind, and while I would prefer ye no' joust if that is—"

Rhiannon laughed and gave him a hearty squeeze around his middle. "I don't need to learn to joust. I think swords and a bow should be sufficient."

"I will see that it is done."

"Now, in the meantime." She glanced back toward the bed. "Perhaps I should test out the comfort of your mighty bed."

Rhiannon broke away from him, strutted over to their bed and flopped down on the mattress. She scooted herself to the middle, reached her arms back and wrapped her fingers around the rings on either end of the headboard.

"My laird," she purred. "Are you going to leave me here all alone?"

Ian swallowed. Like hell he was.

His clothes were shed before he reached the edge of the mattress.

19

Rhiannon woke the next day and swiftly realized it was no longer morning. The sun shone through the opened curtains, and the other half of the bed, where Ian had been after their celebration with the clan last night, was empty. She'd imbibed in wine, and her body still had that wonderful ache of dancing for hours.

She stretched her arms overhead and smiled at the ceiling.

Life as the Countess of Orkney, as Ian's wife, was going to be the most fun and rewarding adventure of her life, she could tell.

Not wanting to waste time lying in bed alone, she tossed her covers aside and climbed out of bed. The floorboards were cold, the air stealing the warmth her toes had absorbed beneath the thick coverlets. She hurried to the basin of water, splashing her face, and began her morning ablutions.

After cleaning herself up, she realized she didn't have anything clean to wear. The gowns she'd been able to borrow had yet to be laundered and had been worn many times. Well, she supposed they could remedy that today. She'd have her clothes washed, and perhaps there was a gown one of the clanswomen would be willing to let her borrow.

Rhiannon dressed in her old gown and opened the door. She was halfway down the stairs when Goosie came tearing up.

Her cat paused and looked up at her, a mouse caught in her jaw.

"Well, I see you've found your first prize."

A bark below had Goosie rushing off. It seemed one of Ian's hounds had also thought to find himself a prize.

Ian was on the heels of his hound, sharply commanding him to stop.

"Ah, good morn, my love," he said, letting momentarily go of the hound's collar long enough for him to take off up the stairs in search of Goosie. "I am terribly sorry about that. The two of them were tearing apart the great hall."

Rhiannon chuckled. "I suppose Goosie and your hound are going to have a wee bit more of a difficult transition than the two of us."

"Aye, Angus is no' fond of cats."

"And Goosie loves to taunt dogs."

"A pair, then."

"Aye."

"Are ye hungry?" Ian asked.

Rhiannon stared at his mouth. "Not for food."

He grinned wickedly. "I promise to satisfy your cravings later, *mo chridhe*, but let us break our fast for now because I want to show ye the isles. The weather is perfect for a long ride."

"I do love the sound of that."

Ian led her into the great hall where their places had been set at the head of the table, two bowls of porridge with fat dollops of melting butter in the center.

After finishing breakfast, they went out to the stable, where their horses were already saddled.

"You knew I'd say aye," she said.

"I'd hoped ye would."

She grinned. "How could I say nay to you?"

"I trust that as time goes on, ye'll recall how to do that. I dinna remember ye shying away when we first were acquainted."

"Very true." She giggled, then ran her hand over the horse's neck and flank. "A gorgeous horse."

"She's yours if ye like the way she rides."

"I'm certain I shall enjoy her immensely."

Cook rushed out toward them, a large leather sack in his hands. "Dinna forget your midday meal, my laird, my lady."

"How splendid," Rhiannon said.

"I expect we'll be back by supper," Ian told the cook. "But if we're no', no need to delay anyone else's meals."

"As ye say, my laird."

They rode through the gates, and Rhiannon's gaze toward the ocean drew her husband's attention.

"Can ye see Noah and Douglass's castle from here?"

"Aye. 'Tis beautiful, but I can see why when you look out, it might have felt isolating here."

"Do ye feel isolated?" His brow wrinkled in concern.

"There's nowhere else I'd rather be."

"Wait until ye see the waterfall. Then ye may change your mind."

"Sounds splendid. Lead the way."

They raced over flat ground and picked their way along the more uneven terrain. Once out of sight of the men on the battlements, Ian pulled their horses to stop often, if only to pull her close for a kiss.

By the time they made it to the waterfall, she was half-mad with wanting of him, but the beauty of it took away her breath.

Nestled in the thickness of the trees was a steaming spring pool with water as clear as fine crystal. What light streamed through the trees made colorful rainbows on the surface, and in the mist of the falls, it poured from a ledge up high down into the pool.

"This is magical," Rhiannon breathed, climbing down from her horse.

"Aye. My favorite place on the isle." He dismounted, took out a blanket and laid it out.

"I can see why." She glanced up at him expectantly. "Can we get in?"

"Aye." He started to unlace his boots, and she followed suit until she stood in her chemise, her bare feet sinking into the mossy ground, and he in only his shirt.

She started to dip a toe into the surprisingly warm water when he said, "Och, nay, remove your chemise."

"We're to swim naked?"

"Is there any other way?" Ian tore off his shirt and dove into the pool as if to prove his point.

Rhiannon stood still, stunned at the strength and build of his physique and his perfect form as he dove in. Was there anything her husband wasn't good at?

He came to the surface, his hair wet against his forehead until he flicked it back.

"Are ye coming, lass?"

"Aye. Though I fear my dive will not be as appealing."

He chuckled. "Everything about ye is appealing to me."

"In that case..." She stripped off her chemise and took a running leap into the water.

Ian was momentarily surprised and then laughed as she landed with a hearty splash beside him. The pool was surprisingly deep, and her feet did not touch the bottom. When she resurfaced, she was beside him. She flashed him a saucy grin, water sluicing off her naked shoulders. And yet she didn't care how exposed she was, not with him.

"Perfect, my love," he said, then wrapped his arms around her and pulled her close, their wet bodies flush in the warm water. His eyes were hooded, his expression full of desire.

She had seen that look before, whenever they kissed, their passions mounting until they were both out of breath. Confidence filled her when he looked at her like that. Her lip curled up in a seductive smile. Ian ran his hands through her hair.

"Ye smell delicious," he whispered as he buried his face in the crook of her neck.

The tingling sensation that only Ian could elicit spread through her body. Her nipples pebbled, and between her legs pulsed with need. She wrapped her arms around his shoulders, hoping, praying he would ease her suffering.

One inviting look from her, and suddenly, he claimed her mouth in a hungry kiss—his lips slanted over hers again and again. She eagerly returned his kisses, measure for measure. He made her feel so good inside. Alive. Her desire heightened, and she rubbed her breasts wantonly against his wet chest. Her belly grew warm, frissons of pleasure stroking her from within.

Beneath the water, the swell of his arousal pressed to her belly. His hands fell to her waist and stroked her skin, and then one hand moved up to cup her breast lightly. His thumb ran gently over her nipple, and she shivered with pleasure at his touch, the feeling raw and sensual as he stroked. She sucked in her breath and then let out a low moan against his mouth. Ian growled low in his throat, deepening their kiss. He pulled her against him tighter, his hands reaching down to grip her buttocks. What heaven was this, bliss in a place that looked like paradise? She moved against him restlessly, his kiss, his touch, all of it making her feel very, *very* good.

Feeling emboldened, she ran her hands down his arms, massaging the muscles that bulged beneath his skin. Her husband was a strong man, a warrior, his body honed and hewed to protect. And she felt safer with him than she had her whole life. She ran her hands along his chest, her thumbs rubbing gently on his nipples, mimicking what he had done to her. At her boldness, he gripped her buttocks harder and lifted her against him, his hard shaft sliding over the crux of her womanhood. She smiled into his mouth at the raw power of passion and how simple, primal movements could make him react.

Continuing her exploration, she ran her hands down the sides of him, slowly edged toward the front and then paused.

Rhiannon's eyes were teasing, her grin seductive.

"Och, woman, ye torment me." Ian crushed his mouth to hers again, fully and deeply. Kissing, licking, nibbling until they were both panting so hard, there was no going back.

Her fingers crushed his rock-hard arousal, and then she gripped him, stroking.

"I canna take this torment," he groaned.

Before she knew what he was doing, Ian lifted her and tossed her over his shoulder, giving her bottom a playful smack. Laughter escaped her, and she playfully pummeled his back. He swam toward the shore and walked out of the spring, carrying her toward their blanket.

Ian laid her out and stood over her for several heartbeats, gaze roving hungrily, possessively over her body.

Rhiannon swallowed hard, her mouth suddenly dry. Ian was fully aroused, large, and swollen. The sheer size of him would be daunting if she didn't already know how good he could make her feel. Rhiannon slowly let her gaze rise to his face, and she sucked in her breath at the intensity with which he looked at her. His gaze spoke of the things they'd done, the promises of more.

"Make love to me, Ian."

He drew in a quick breath, dropped to his knees, and slid the length of his body over hers. He pulled her closer with his hands running through her hair, deepening their kiss. He parted her lips with his tongue and thrust it inside, imitating the ancient lovemaking ritual.

She pressed against him, sighing into his mouth, until he pulled his mouth from hers and made soft kisses down her throat, flicking her skin with his tongue.

"Mmm..." she moaned.

Warmth spread through her limbs, and she was aware only of the hot, velvet tongue that lapped at her flesh and made her envision wicked things.

When his mouth settled on her nipple, flicking back and forth before suckling it, she thought she would leap from her skin. She arched her back and, at the same time, thrust her hips against him. His hard erection pressed the apex of her thighs with a delicious spark. She wanted him to sink inside her.

"Rhiannon, ye dinna know what ye do to me," he said hoarsely. He pulled away to gaze into her eyes.

"If it's anything like what you do to me...I know all too well." Her voice was just as hoarse, her breath coming in pants.

His smile was wicked, and Rhiannon laughed, lightning flashing through her body. They would end the torment here and now.

Ian leaned down and kissed her gently and softly, sucking her bottom lip into his mouth. He caressed her arms up and down with the backs of his fingers and then came to rest at her waist, one thumb circling her navel, as his mouth tenderly placed soft, wet kisses on her neck and shoulders.

He took his time, making love to her with the soft pads of his fingers and the light, feathery touch of his mouth on her skin.

The gentle torture of his touch drove Rhiannon to the brink of ecstasy. She clutched at him, desperate for more. The weight of his body, the hardness of his arousal, sent white-hot waves of pleasure through her.

Ian slowly moved against her. Sparks of lightning flashed each time he glided forward, his hard member rubbing against the sensitive spot, damp with wanting.

Rhiannon clung to him as he imitated the act of making love. Frissons of need grew from tiny sparks to a blazing inferno. She wanted him. Wanted him deep inside her.

He moved lower. His tongue made lazy circles down her throat to the tops of her breasts. His body kept its rhythmic motion, sliding over and over, as his mouth moved to nuzzle the valley between her breasts, his tongue deliberately toying with her in seductive moves. Licking, sucking, nipping at everything but the pink tip that begged for his ardent attention.

She cried out when he finally pulled her nipple into his mouth, slowly sucking it in and out, his tongue teasing her. The pleasure and pressure within her built as his mouth made love to her breasts, and his body pushed against her core. She wrapped her legs around his hips, lifting so the tip of his cock pressed to her core, begging for more.

Ian groaned at her movement and then shifted himself. The warmth of his heated body left, only to be replaced by him kissing her belly, his tongue circling her navel, and then lower still. As he kissed the inside of her thighs, he nipped lightly at the sensitive skin there. Oh, heaven help her, the decadent feelings his mouth elicited made her body thrum with pleasure.

She nearly fainted from the memory of his mouth on her

most delicate place. Before she could think more about it, his mouth covered her sex. Rhiannon cried out, her fingers pressing into the hard muscles of his shoulders.

His tongue flicked up and down, in and out, sending flames to spread through her. Her legs shook from sheer pleasure, and when she thought it couldn't get any better, her body exploded.

"Ian!" she cried out, her hips coming off the ground, her hands holding his head to the very heat of her.

When the waves of pleasure subsided, she stared at Ian, in awe of the passion they ignited together.

She kissed him, her tongue flicking around his lips. He growled low in his throat as she slowly trailed her lips from his, placing seductive kisses from his cheek to his neck.

"I'm going to kiss you like you kiss me," she breathed into his ear.

He moaned into her ear. "Och, aye, *mo chridhe.*"

She kissed him gently on his shoulders, her hands running up and down his chest as she kissed from his neck to his navel, paying attention to each of his nipples that stood as erect as hers.

She traveled the muscled length of his abdomen, circling his navel and grinning at his sharp intakes of breath and soft moans. With one hand fisted in the blanket, his other gently gripped the back of her head. Her confidence spiked, and she grew bolder. Moving lower, she lightly scratched down the length of his muscular thighs. She kissed his thighs, massaging the sinewy muscle, and then she traveled northward again, reaching his swollen member—the target all along. She licked from base to tip and kissed the top before wrapping her lips around the head. Having already done this before, she knew exactly what he liked. She sucked lightly and then moved down and up. His moans increased, and his hips bucked as she spread the same fire of pleasure he had with the velvety movements of her tongue.

She worked his length with her hand, her mouth meeting each stroke.

"Oh, God, Rhiannon..."

His moans spurred her on, and she sucked harder, faster, moaning against his thick length. His legs shook, and his grip upon her hair grew tighter, hips pumping with increased vigor. Then he cried out, his body stiffening, and she jerked his shaft from her mouth, warm fluid spilling over her hands.

Rhiannon grinned at him, fully satisfied to have been able to bring him to the point of shattering.

"Ye are an amazing and beautiful woman, wife." He returned her grin.

"And you, Earl of Orkney, are an amazing, handsome man." She lay beside him, trailing her fingers over his chest as he slowly caressed her hip. "Do I please you?"

"Och, aye, ye please me much. And what about me? Do I make a good husband?" He nuzzled against her neck.

She sucked in her breath at the feel of his mouth on her skin again, flames of heat igniting again so soon.

"I am more than pleased, Ian. You are everything I dreamed of," she whispered.

"And ye are the only woman in the world who could break my vow of bachelorhood."

Rhiannon laughed. "'Tis glad I am, or we'd have a problem."

Ian laughed and rolled her onto her back, trapping her body with his. "Nay, no problems here."

20

One month later
Balla Dorcha Castle, Orkney Isles

R hiannon wiped the sweat from her brow. Ian was not letting up on her today, and she was glad for it. Every challenge brought out a new and improved skill from her.

"Your swordsmanship is superb, *mo chridhe*."

His heart, she certainly loved the sound of that.

"Again," she said, returning to a fighting stance.

Ian grinned, circling her, his wooden sword held out. Funny, he fought with that and allowed her to use a real sword so she could understand the weapon's weight.

"My laird." Their practice was interrupted by Mac, who was newly back from his voyage to Ireland to return the men who'd been recovering from the shipwreck since their ship had been unrepairable in the end.

"Aye, Mac?" Ian said, poking the tip of his wooden sword into the rushes of the great hall.

"A signal from Caithness. *The* signal."

"Noah?" Ian's brow creased with concern. Being only a short sail from each other and with Rhiannon and Douglass wanting to get together often, they had only just returned from Caithness a few days ago. Douglass had gone into labor, and Rhiannon had wanted to be there, aiding her cousin in delivering a healthy son.

But the signal was as ominous as it sounded.

Ian charged from the great hall with Rhiannon in his wake, to see the dark smoke curling into the air across the sea. Thick black clouds visible even from hear meant massive flames. Was that the signal? Signal for what? An attack?

"Fok," Ian growled.

"What is it?" Rhiannon's voice shook with fear as she gripped onto Ian's arm and stared in the direction of the dark smoke signal across the water. Douglass... the infant.... She crossed herself and murmured a prayer.

"War." The declaration dripped from Ian's mouth in one angry syllable.

Rhiannon glanced up at her husband, her blood running cold. Ian's mouth was pinched, his muscles tense. The warrior she'd seen before come to the surface.

"Thank ye, Mac."

When he looked back down at her now, his face was stricken. "I need to go to Buanaiche. Now. That smoke, it means they're under attack."

"Attack..." The word came out slowly, softly. "Will you be able to make it in time?"

"I dinna know. That signal means a siege has already begun." Ian let out a low curse.

"I'm going with you."

"What? Nay. Ye must remain behind. For your safety."

"Nay, Ian. I'm not going to remain safe here on an isle when you are not safe."

"That is the way of things. I canna risk ye being injured. Or worse."

Rhiannon's heart stuttered in her chest, panic rising. "Douglass, her infant, they will need me."

"I will have no way to get ye into the castle without opening the gate and letting the enemy in as well. Ye'll put them in more danger than helping."

Rhiannon started to tremble. Ian going to war. Noah going to war. Douglass and her sweet, innocent babe, in the midst of it. She could hardly breathe with the fear of it.

"Who are they fighting?" For a moment, she feared it was her brother's army coming back for him. "Could they be here for Adam?"

"I dinna know. But I need to leave immediately."

Ian barked orders for the ship to be ready, for his men to prepare for battle. For Adam to be shackled and loaded onto the ship.

Within a quarter hour, his army was marching up the gangway of the ship, and Ian was at the base. Adam's cursing could be heard even from here, though he was in the bowels of the vessel. There was only one way to resolve the issue if that was their purpose, and killing him wasn't an option.

Rhiannon threw herself into her husband's arms, staring back at Balla Dorcha, the castle they'd made their home, and worried she might never experience the joy she had these last few months.

"Dinna fash, my love," Ian said. "I will return, hale and hearty, and continue your training. Continue everything." He pressed a kiss to her forehead, then tipped her chin, kissing her lips.

"I'm scared. And I hate that feeling."

"I will prevail. I always do."

"But what—"

"Nay, lass, dinna think anything but."

She nodded, forcing her mind to repeat over and over that he would prevail. That he would return to her in one piece, and they would return together to their life on the isle. That when he did, perhaps they would conceive a child, which had yet to occur despite their vigorous attempts.

"Sinclairs are victorious," she said and hugged him tight, not wanting to let go.

"Always. We dinna know how no' to be." Ian's composure fell for a split second, emotion clouding his eyes. "My love. *Mo chridhe.*"

Rhiannon wrapped her arms around him, her head pressed to his heart. "Come back to me."

"Soon." He kissed her softly, then more deeply, a promise to return.

"I love you so much," she said.

"I love ye, too, my darling lass. And I promise, the time I'm away will fly, and when I'm home again, I will no' leave your side until I'm forced."

She smiled. "That sounds perfect to me."

Ian looked pained for a moment as he held her. "If I were a god, I'd send a bolt of lightning to vanquish our enemies so that I didna have to leave ye."

"I believe you would. And I'm glad you're as loyal as you are. Your brother is very lucky to have you. And so am I." She personally knew what it was like to have a sibling who wasn't honorable, who would betray her at the first chance he got.

"Your brother is lucky to have ye too, lass. I'd have killed him." He chuckled.

Rhiannon giggled and gave him a playful punch in the ribs. "Go on now, before I don't let you leave."

Ian tugged her into his arms one last time, giving her a mind-blowing kiss.

"To remember me by."

"To look forward to what happens next," she added.

"Aye, love." And then he was walking away, joining his warriors on the ship. He stopped, turned once more. "I love ye."

"I love you, too." It was an effort not to run forward, to grab hold of him. And when they set sail, she dashed to the edge of the water, and would have tossed herself in to swim after him if it hadn't been for Mac who took hold of her elbow.

"He'll be back, my lady. Dinna fash."

She had to trust that, even if her heart was screaming no.

The ship became a speck on the horizon, barely noticeable, but what remained was the thick black smoke and her fear.

"It willna be long, my lady," Mac said, giving her arm a gentle squeeze of comfort. "Together, the Sinclairs are liable to mow down the enemy within a quarter-hour. Might even be home in time for a midnight dram."

"I will wish for that every second he's away."

"Your husband is famous in Scotland," Mac said. "A legend among men. Ye've nothing to fear."

Rhiannon nodded, her shoulders sagging and she leaned against the older seneschal. The only thing that would distract her was planning the celebration for when her husband returned. For there was no question of if, only when.

WHEN THEY ARRIVED AT THE SHORES OF HIS BROTHER'S land, Ian still didn't have a clear view of the enemy, but worried they would have seen him coming. They dropped anchor, rowed out to the shore, with arms that were swift.

They leapt from their rowboats and ran stealthily toward

the castle, all the while his senses keen for any sign of the enemy. In the distance, he could hear the loud crack of thunder, but the sky was blue. It wasn't weather that made that sound, but a massive boulder as it flung from a trebuchet and smacked against the stones of Buanaiche Castle.

Battle-rush coursed through his veins, and his palms itched against the hilt of his sword with the need to run their enemies through. They were only just over a rise from the beach when he took in the army at his brother's gates.

He let out a battle cry that shook the earth, and ran toward the enemy at full force.

With his men beside him, they leaped into fighting the enemy from behind while his brother's army assaulted from the front.

"Get to that trebuchet," Ian shouted to his second, who nodded and hacked his way through the throng.

They were English, there was no doubt by their clothes, their thick chainmail armor, and the insults made more insulting by their accents.

A dozen *Sassenachs* surged forward, egged on by a man on horseback—the man who had tried to steal Ian's bride. He couldn't recall the name, or if he'd ever been given one, but Arsehole seemed to fit him well.

The clanging of metal and shouts of pain echoed through the land just outside the castle. On the battlements, Matilda and Iliana shot arrows. And from a window—not just any window, from Noah and Douglass's bedchamber—arrows shot through and landed in the enemy's hearts. Douglass was not going to go down without a fight.

Two attacked Ian from behind and Ian whirled, hacking at their chainmail. He cut one down with his claymore, and then another. Swinging his massive sword in a wide arc until he was clearing a path for his own men to get closer.

His second reached the trebuchet, and with a mighty

thwack cut through the rope pulley system, rendering the deadly instrument useless.

Ian made his way through the throngs of battling men, cutting this way and that, until he was face to face with the villain.

"We can give ye Adam," Ian said as they circled one another, the rest of the fighting men staying back. "He's on our ship. Take him and leave."

"'Tis not Adam I want," Arsehole sneered. "I have come back for my bride."

"She's no' yours. I have wedded her. Bedded her. Ye'll never have her."

"I will if I make her a widow this day."

"Ye willna leave here alive, unless it is with Adam on the ship."

Arsehole snorted, spat on the ground narrowly missing Ian's boot. "You think your savage army is going to be able to hold up to mine? My men are more refined."

"Refinement is the last thing needed on the field of battle."

"Is that so? Then what is it you think necessary to win?"

"Strength. Cunning. Skill."

Arsehole laughed. "Cunning, that's a good one. You may have strength." He pointed his sword at Ian's arm's indicating the size. "And skill," he glanced around at the obvious destruction. "But cunning you lack."

"Only a weak man feels the need to insult another man's intelligence."

"Is that not what you did?"

"Nay. Ye asked what I thought it took."

The Arsehole narrowed his eyes. "Then to the death."

"If that is your wish. Where shall we send your remains?"

"You won't have need of that." Arsehole cocked his arm, looking almost like he was going to throw his sword at Ian, a fighting stance he'd not seen before that made him wonder if either the man was mad, or had discovered some new and improved way of fighting.

Unfortunately, it appeared to be the former.

Arsehole rushed him, and Ian easily stepped aside, put out his foot and the imbecile went sprawling, narrowly missing running himself through by an inch.

"Are ye certain ye dinna want to take me up on my offer? We would escort ye to the ship and allow ye and Adam to leave without issue."

The man sputtered and leaped to his feet, surprisingly agile considering the thick chainmail on his person. Perhaps he was simply tired.

"Never!" Arsehole ran toward Ian again, sword out, spittle on his lips.

Once more, Ian dodged, put out his foot and the bastard went flying, this time into a group of men busy hacking at each other, who tossed him backward. Ian caught him on the back, steadied him and retreated a distance from Arsehole's sword.

"It's never too late," Ian offered again. "Happy to let ye leave. All ye have to do is issue the order for your men to cease their fighting."

No words came from Arsehole this time, simply a growl and a shout and he *did* throw his sword. Incredibly stupid. Ian ducked and the weapon sailed over his head, landing in one of the other Englishmen.

"That was bad form, mate," Ian said with a frown.

The Arsehole rushed him, weaponless, completely out of his mind. Ian swung with a fist, clocked him on the chin with an arched hit upward and watched him fall in an unconscious heap.

"Idiot." It wasn't fair to kill a man when he was down, so Ian simply turned to the other warring men, letting a piercing whistle escape his throat. "Your leader has been taken down!" They didn't need to know he was merely unconscious. "Surrender or die!"

Several dozen *Sassenachs* paused in their fighting, looked at one another, and then dropped to their knees.

"Smart lads," Ian said. "This is over. Dinna come back here again. I thought I'd made that clear the last time we met."

Noah pushed through the crowd to stand beside Ian. He held out his hand and Ian gripped it.

"Signal works," Noah grinned.

"I'm sorry to have brought this on ye."

"Ah, we needed the exercise."

Ian stared toward the ruined wall by the front gate. "I'll help ye rebuild."

"Only if ye bring your wife. If Douglass sees ye here, but no' Rhiannon, I'll never hear the end of it."

"We have an accord." Ian clapped his brother on the back, giving him a manly hug.

"If ye're quite finished, this is a hell of a mess we need to clean up." The shout came from Iliana on the battlements, and despite the shrewish words, her voice was full of laughter.

All of them were relieved it was over, and that it had ended in victory, with no losses on their side.

They spent the next several hours burying the dead, tending the wounded, and making sure the castle was at least fortified for the night. Adam's idiot cohort was locked in the dungeon, and screaming obscenities—Adam right beside him.

"I'll be back tomorrow," Ian said. Though he was exhausted, he knew if he didn't sail home tonight, Rhiannon would be going mad on the other side. And he did not want her to worry another moment. "Want me to take the prisoners back to the isle?"

"Nay, no' necessary. When ye come back, we'll make a

plan to return them to their rightful homeland. Though truly, they deserve a much worse punishment."

"Maybe we drop them just shy of the border?"

"Make them fight their way across?"

Ian chuckled. "They made it this far, seems fair."

"When you come back, bring your wife," Douglass ordered.

"Ye have my word, my lady."

Not too long after, Ian was leaping off the side of the ship and swimming to shore in the dark.

A figure rushed him, and from the size and shape, he knew it was her—his beautiful, charming, lovely wife—Rhiannon.

"Oh, my darling." She kissed him all over his face, her hands pressed to his cheeks, checking his chest for wounds. "I was so scared. I'm so glad you're back. Oh, I didn't think I could take another moment's torment."

Ian wrapped her in his arms. "I promised ye I'd return."

"I knew you would."

"In time for a midnight dram," Mac called from a few feet away.

"A midnight dram, and so much more." Ian lifted his wife in his arms and carried her back inside, to their home. "Our adventures have only just begun."

EPILOGUE

F *ive years later...*
Balla Dorcha Castle, Orkney Isles

RHIANNON RACED ACROSS THE MOORS ON THE ISLE—ON foot.

Oh, she had become quite fast in the years she'd been wed to Ian. Whether it was a race up the stairs to their bedroom, a race across the beach to see who could reach the water first, or a race after their two small girls, Rhea and Isla, they were constantly in movement.

This was the life she'd always wanted.

This was the life she'd been gifted.

Pure happiness.

And pure speed.

"Mama, so fast!" Shouted Rhea on her back.

"No! Dada so fast!" Ian broke in front of her, Isla clinging to his broad shoulders, as he sped forward the way she imagined he did on the fields of battle when he was called away.

And there had been many, but he always returned. Hale and hearty, and more passionate for her than the day he left. As if any moment spent away from her made his love and desire for her increase tenfold. He a starving warrior, and she the feast that healed.

"Mama, faster." Rhea's little hands pounded her shoudlers as if doing so would make her suddenly gain wings to fly. Rhiannon wouldn't discount that. In moments like this, surrounded by her husband, her children, in a cloud of love and joy, she did feel like she was soaring.

"I'm... trying..." she laughed through her panting, picking up her pace.

Ian was always faster. He had longer legs, more practive. But she wasn't too far behind. She never was. And there were plenty of days when she raced him after he'd been through a full day of training that she won.

Like today.

Their feet hit the sand of the beach, and Ian faltered, though it was only a second, it was enough that Rhiannon was able to get in the lead. And the isle provided, for the sea rushed up on the beach to met her, and she was the first with wet feet—which mean she'd won.

"We won!" shouted Rhea, her tiny heels kicking against Rhiannon's ribs.

"I wanted to win," pouted Isla.

"We all win," Rhiannon said, setting down the little imp.

The two girls rushed off and Ian wrapped his arms around Rhiannon. "They are wrong. I am the one who won five years ago."

"Nay, husband, it is I who have won." It was an argument they played out daily, and not one they were bound to ever agree on.

But that made it all the more fun, for in truth, they *had* both won, and that much was clearly evident.

Their love was a victory, and their life the very adventure they both had sought.

ABOUT THE AUTHOR

Eliza Knight is an award-winning and USA Today bestselling author.

Her love of history began as a young girl when she traipsed the halls of Versailles and ran through the fields in Southern France. She can still remember standing before the great golden palace, and imagining what life must have been like. Join Eliza (sometimes as E.) on riveting historical journeys that cross landscapes around the world.

While not reading, writing or researching for her latest book, she chases after her three children. In her spare time (if there is such a thing...) she likes daydreaming, wine-tasting, traveling, hiking, staring at the stars, watching movies, shopping and visiting with family and friends.

She is the creator of the popular historical blog, History Undressed and a co-host on the History, Books and Wine podcast.

She lives atop a small mountain with her own knight in shining armor, three princesses, two very naughty Newfies, and a turtle named Fish.

Visit Eliza at http://www.elizaknight.com or her historical blog History Undressed: www.historyundressed.com. Sign up for her newsletter to get news about books, events, contests and sneak peaks: https://elizaknight.com/news/!

facebook.com/elizaknightfiction

x.com/elizaknight

instagram.com/elizaknightfiction

bookbub.com/authors/eliza-knight

goodreads.com/elizaknight

Printed in Great Britain
by Amazon